# ZABIBA AND THE KING

## By its author
## Saddam Hussein

### Edited by Robert Lawrence

"Zabiba and the King," edited by Robert Lawrence. ISBN 1-58939-585-9.

Published 2004 by Virtualbookworm.com Publishing Inc., P.O. Box 9949, College Station, TX 77845, US. ©2004, Robert Lawarence. All rights reserved. No part of this publication may be reproduced, stored in a retrieval system, or transmitted in any form or by any means, electronic, mechanical, recording or otherwise, without the prior written permission of Robert Lawrence.

Manufactured in the United States of America.

Figure 1

# PREFACE

Written just 3 years prior to the launch of Operation Iraqi Freedom, this work is actually the first of at least three novels authored by Saddam Hussein. Its translation from Arabic into English is a project by the editor, a native born U.S. citizen, for the benefit of the curious, the patriotic, the educator, the historian, etc., as well as for the friends and families of those serving in Iraq.

**WHAT IS THE BOOK ABOUT AND WHY WAS THE CIA SO INTERESTED IN IT?** This novel titled, "Zabiba And The King," is an allegorical love story between a mighty king (*Saddam*) and a simple, yet beautiful commoner named Zabiba (*the Iraqi people*), [as narrated by a wise old village woman to the children gathered around a campfire]. Zabiba is married to a cruel, unloving husband who repeatedly forces himself upon her against her will, (*the United States and Collation forces*), and finally rapes her and beats her mercilessly. This act of rape is compared to the invasion by foreign troops onto the soil of a sovereign state (*United States and Collation forces invasion of Iraq*). The marriage of Zabiba to her husband was strictly an economic arrangement negotiated out of economic necessity by Zabiba's father and to fulfill the wicked lust of the husband. (*The Iraqi people have a relationship with the United States and the other countries represented by the Collation forces only out of economic necessity and not by choice*). According to numerous U.S. newspaper articles that appeared in May, 2001, CIA officials were reported to have said that the book was a unique opportunity to study Saddam's thinking process. Reportedly, the CIA analyzed and scrutinized the book from cover to cover, even trying to read in between the lines.

**WHERE IS THE SETTING?** It is not clear where the setting of the various dialogues between Zabiba and the king take place, beyond his palace, her hut and on the road in between. We are given no other geographic landmarks, but it is definitely assumed to be inside Iraq. However, the setting of the storytelling of the wise old woman is in a village on the bank of the River Zab. In Northern Iraq, the Tigris River flows from Northwest to Southeast through the city of Mosul and then through the capitol of Baghdad some 250 miles downstream. There are two Zab Rivers that empty into the Tigris flowing from the direction of the mountainous region along the Iraq - Iran border, the Great Zab and the Little Zab. The Great Zab deposits into the Tigris just below Mosul near the ancient city of Nineveh. The Little Zab intersects the Tigris approximately 65 miles North of the town of Tikrit. Just North of Tikrit, but below the Little Zab, on the Western bank of the Tigris is Jebel Makhul, the Black Mountain. The purpose of the geography lesson is to point out that the location of the village where this story is being told is within close proximity of the stomping grounds of a young Saddam Hussein. Saddam was born in the tiny village of Al-Auja, on the outskirts of Tikrit. He lived there with his mother and an abusive stepfather until he was 10 years old. His small village was very close to the village of the old woman in the story. Tikrit was [until late 2003] the center of Iraq's ruling elite. Saddam reportedly has one of his palaces constructed on Black Mountain overlooking the Tigris.

**WHAT IS THE TIME SETTING?** If Saddam was reminiscing of stories told by his grandmother, the time setting of the storytelling would likely be before his eighteenth birthday, [making it between 1937, the year of his birth, and 1955. It is also common knowledge that at the age of eighteen, after completing primary school, Saddam left the area of Tikrit with his uncle's family and moved to Baghdad to enter the Al-Karkh secondary school.] The era of the story being told by the old woman appears to be in the mid-600's to early 700's AD, as the main character, Zabiba, is a devout follower of Islam, yet the king still worships the idols of his forefathers and is ignorant of some of the fundamental traditions of the Islamic faith. [Mohammed founded the religion in around 610 AD and he died in 632 AD]. The author makes brief reference to the Jews, Jesus Christ, Abraham, Noah, Adam and Eve, Nineveh, Assyria and Babylon.

**DID SADDAM HUSSEIN REALLY WRITE THE NOVEL?** One of the things that makes this book so interesting to read is that one finds himself at different points in the book, questioning whether or not Saddam Hussein could have written it or not. One argument some have suggested against his authorship is that they feel the writer is a little too *in tune* to the character Zabiba's female emotions and psyche. On the other hand, the release of this book in the original language was an overnight best seller in Iraq and even became an on-stage musical production. Everyone in Iraq believes that Saddam is the author. Even though he had many opportunities, he refused to deny that he wrote it. And since the book promotes the establishment of a quasi-democratic form of government whereby a "people's council" made up of common citizens that advise the ruler, it is the editor's opinion that such a book would not have been allowed to be published in Iraq, much less performed on-stage in Baghdad, unless Saddam Hussein were somehow intimately involved in its creation. The book also boldly suggests that the ruler's sons should not automatically succeed the ruler upon his death. Based on common knowledge of Saddam's sons, Uday and Ussay, it would be hard to believe that such brutal men would tolerate such propaganda...unless, of course, it was written by dear ol' dad.

**WHAT PROBLEMS WERE ENCOUNTERED DURING TRANSLATION?** Within certain practical limits, every effort was made to produce as accurate a translation as possible. In some instances the original Arabic conveyed the same concept or idea two, three and four times within the same sentence or adjacent sentences. In such cases the redundancy was limited to at most twice. Also in the Arabic, two or more unrelated, or loosely related, ideas were frequently conveyed within a single sentence. In an effort to maintain accuracy some of the resulting sentences in the English are wordy and somewhat cumbersome. The reasons for this have more to do with the distinctiveness of the two languages and cultures, rather than the ability of the translators or even the author. Another problem encountered was the depth of layered quotes within the text...on at least one occasion, four deep. The narration by the author and his comments outside of the story line are represented in italics. Narration by the old woman in telling her story is presented without quotation marks. And dialogue between characters within the story line are depicted with traditional open and closed quotation marks.

# Introduction[1]

On February 12, 2000, our president and leader Saddam Hussein, may Allah keep and protect him, met with the writers of Iraq. He exhorted them to write novels that would describe all aspects of human life, so that every author would try to draw a parallel between everyday life and the events described in their novels, raising the courage of those who are fighting armed with anti-aircraft guns against the planes of the enemy.

He said, "Right now, we need to create works so deep that the reader would find in the history, social life and psychology of a human being something he had never known before, no matter what the subject of the story might be: the deeds of a woman or a man, an old man or a youth, sick or recovering, a soldier who comes home on leave, with all that he feels as he comes back from the front, or as he leaves home to go back to the battle.

"It is also necessary that the reader, having been introduced to such works and having understood the main idea and having connected it to thoughts about all varieties of this life, could in turn pass what had become available for his understanding on to others."

This brilliant idea inspired Nadjib Gujur,* one of the honorable sons of Iraq, and as a result came into existence this novel that the reader is holding in his hands right now. Yet because of modesty, usual for all sons of Iraq, who prefer to sacrifice themselves rather than talk of great deeds that are being done by their hands, the author preferred that his name did not appear on the cover of this book.

---

* *EDITOR'S NOTE:* Gujur - means "the Jealous One."

That is why it says here: A novel of its author.

[1] ***EDITOR'S NOTE:*** The "Introduction" is presented without changes from the original Arabic. The Editor chose to release the novel under the real name of the author [i.e. Saddam Hussein].

# Zabiba And The King

*H*ow many strange and unusual things, how many heroic and glorious deeds, how many true wonders occur in Iraq?

*Is not life in the midst of ordinary things filled with the most extraordinary things? Is its consistent flow not interrupted by some unexpected leaps? Could the colors of life be rich if the most ordinary things were not interspersed with miracles? Would a valley bring delight to the eyes of the one gazing at it if there were no mountain peaks above it?*

*Is a state not defined by its opposite, and color by the bordering shades? Is a high mountain not distinguished by the background of a valley that surrounds it? Does not Iraq and all that was and is in Iraq since the beginning of time lie between the heavens and the earth?*

*Is it not here, and nowhere else, that the construction of the building of an incredible height, stretching from the earth to the heavens, took place? The foundation cracked under the weight of its walls when the heavens burst forth in wrath; and the top of the building and what was between the top and the foundation collapsed, and only a portion of the walls remained standing, thrust towards the sky (as it happened to the legendary Ziggurat\* in Abu Harib, which was being built in the beginning of the 15th century BC).*

---

\* **EDITOR'S NOTE:** Ziggurat – comes from the Babylonian word Zigguratu – "the top." It was the temple dome portion of the temple buildings of the Babylonian and Assyrian civilizations.

Is it not here, and here alone, that one of the Seven Wonders of the World – the hanging gardens of Babylon – was? If everything were judged honestly half of the monuments called the Wonders of the World could have been on the grounds of Iraq.*

Was it not by the will of Allah that Adam and Eve were sent to the Iraqi land? Was it not here that Abraham was born, may he rest in peace? Is it not with Iraq that all the prophets and prophecies were concerned, from the prophet Abraham to the very last prophet whose name, let it be blessed, was Muhammad?

Is not Iraq with its mountains and its plateau of An Najaf the homeland of the prophet Noah, may he rest in peace, in the times after the prophet Adam, may he rest in peace?

Would anybody be surprised by anything unusual or extraordinary, if this unusual thing were coming out of Iraq?

Is it not in Iraq where the missionary spirit of the people rose up, saturated with the aroma of prophecies and divine grace? Otherwise, what would tie those who live today with those who shed their blood when they went into eternity before and during the Mother of All Battles? Those heroes died so that the banner of the Islamic nation might again be upheld after it had been marred by the agents of the enemy and those worthless infidels, casting shame upon the whole nation when the raging Zionism burst forth and formed a grotesque alliance with America. Now it became almost impossible to imagine that the horror of the enslavement of the whole

---

* **EDITOR'S NOTE:** The seven wonders of the ancient world include: 1) Hanging Gardens of Babylon (Iraq), 2) The Great Pyramid of Giza (Egypt), 3) The Lighthouse of Alexandra (Egypt), 4) The Colossus of Rhodes (Greece), 5) The Mausoleum at Halicarnassus (Turkey), 6) The Temple of Artemis at Ephesus (Turkey), and 7) The Statue of Zeus at Olympia (Greece). The editor assumes that the author believes that Egypt should be part of Iraq!

*world by this alliance could ever come to an end and that resistance to this alliance could ever bring any positive results. The sense of defeat that this alliance brought not only struck those in power, but also weakened those whose names had just recently been on the lists of the most progressive and revolutionary parties, movements, and individuals!*

*Is it not surprising and comparable to a miracle that Iraq rose up, saddled his horse, unsheathed his sword and cried out, "I am Iraq, the only one in the whole Earth, declaring firmly, for all to hear: 'You, Brutality and Lawlessness, stay where you are or retreat! This is the land of prophets and heavenly utterances!'" As Allah was looking upon him from the height of the heavens, Iraq thundered in a loud voice: "We shall not bend our knee before any but Allah! Let all the cowards, compromisers, and traitors get out. We shall not capitulate! Let all the Arabs who have forgotten that they are the descendants of Yarub and that they worship Allah alone get out!"*

*Iraq was the country of prophets and revelations, the country of civilizations, of merchantry, and of purity, where the first plants sprouted and milk flowed from the udder, so that there was life and so that there was the world in all its virgin purity and sins, with all the sweetness and bitterness of life. Iraq has been the land from which the door opens to heaven for those who rise there and to hell for those who are destined to burn in its flames.*

*Iraq – the land of Sumer and Akkadia, Babylon and Assyria, established civilizations, Baghdad and Samarra, the country of famous hawks and noble beauties, a land without which there would be no sun, and without which the moon would not find its way in the sky; nor would plants sprout to the joy of the farmer and to the envy of infidels, nor would there be rain.*

*In the Iraqi land, in its natural state, rich with stories about heroic and glorious deeds, famous for examples of architecture and of faith, in its valleys and in its mountains, on its lakes, where the Polar Star and Saturn reflect in the moonlight, you will see many things amazing and worthy of awe.*

*In Iraq it is not customary to tell vain tales and jokes. "Whether true or not, once upon a time," is how the old woman from the village where my family lived would start her stories. Because she had a great mind and common wisdom, all the villagers, men and women, came to her to ask for her advice. Besides, she nursed all their illnesses, and all the boys and girls loved her. Both young and old listened to her stories and lessons. Here is what she once told:*

Long, long ago there was a powerful and proud king. His glory spread far and brought him respect, well-being, love, and loyalty from his followers, as well as reverence and fear from those who were afraid of him. This was even before the time when Allah decided to draw the line between that which is now considered allowed and that which is forbidden through his prophets. It was also before people began to revere Allah's law, decrees, statutes, and traditions with the devotion they had later. People would submit to the king, some out of good will and some by force, and he became the king of his time, the king of the four corners of the earth. He wanted people who lived far from the place where his throne stood and where his power was revered to bow their heads before him. He wanted kings that ruled in the far reaches of the ancient world to submit to him, so that they would govern their people under his name while revering him.

*The old woman interrupted her story and went about doing one of her many chores for this* *winter evening while we sat around the fire, though it could only warm those who could get close enough to it. I did not understand the meaning of that story, but I knew the old woman very well and knew that she was wiser then all others in our village, a settlement on the bank of the river Zab to the northeast of the black mountain\* (Makhul) and the eastern bank of the river Tigris above the city of Ash-Sharqat, where the ruins of ancient Assyria, founded 3,000 years before Christ, in the times of the first Assyrian era, remain.*

*I knew that Grandmother always found stories with a moral for us. Some of them she would make up herself; others she drew from the rich inheritance of the people. She would add some things and leave out others so that the meaning of the story would take shape in the way that she intended for us to hear it, and so that the stories would have just the effect on us that she wanted them to have. In that, she was not at all different from other grandmothers who raise boys and girls, the children of their daughters and the children of their sons. In each of her stories she would point our attention to what we should avoid in life and what we should pursue, and each story had its moral and goal.*

*All grandmothers and uncles and aunts who were older than our mothers would tell stories like that. While handing down to us stories, proverbs, and other wisdom, they were a substitute for television. Oh, if television would give us even a hundredth of the education that we have received from their lips! Some old men were storytellers who sat in their yards or houses, where they shared the same kind of stories, which bear lessons of courage and*

---

\* **EDITOR'S NOTE:** Saddam Hussein reportedly has one of his palaces located on Black Mountain overlooking the Tigris.

pass on the good traditions of the previous genera-
tions to the children and youths?

*Our wise storyteller continued her narrative:*

"The king got bored with his lonely existence
at the palace and, feeling sorrow in his soul, he
rode out of the city into the fields. From afar he saw
an imposing palace. The king and his courtiers rode
for about half an hour (that is, if we measure time
the way they do it in our days) at times whipping
the horses and at times riding at a normal gait,
when he realized that the palace was comparable to
his, only just slightly smaller. The king asked whom
the palace belonged to and found out that it belonged to a rich merchant, who enjoyed friendship
with a great multitude of governors and gave many
rich receptions in that palace. As to the fields and
lands, they had been granted to him and his father
by one of the kings of the past."

*Here, our wise story-teller, as if it were a joke,
said:*

*Isn't it true, that the friends of rulers who give
lavish banquets and those who accept their invita-
tions to sit at their tables, carry the grand titles of
rich merchants, landowners, influential people, and
prosperous tradesmen? Isn't it true that rulers are
especially generous to the people who are not of the
people? Aren't the kings generous with only the people's money when they give it to those who are rich,
my children? Or maybe you think that you might get
something from their generosity? So, that is how that
prior king blessed the merchant by giving him that
palace, and you are left here with your grandma in
this shack that barely withstands the wintry winds
with its roof that leaks at even the hint of rain!*

*She said that and burst out laughing. And be-
ing the naughty children we are, we started laughing
when we saw her toothless mouth. Only a few of her*

*teeth had not been destroyed by time, and even those left were crooked and worn down.*

*As she was telling of kings and their riches, it was if she were chewing words. Every word swirled on her lips for some time until it became audible, as if she were weighing whether or not each word was fitting for the story. And then, when she would re-member how she was betrothed to her cousin and how she received a dowry of fewer than a dozen sheep which were immediately taken by her father, who did not leave any to her and did not even buy her a new dress, she was taken by grief, even though it had happened almost forty years ago.*

*We had to remind our storyteller of reality so that she would return from her own story to the story of the king, and she continued on:*

The king was surprised when he was told all about the merchant, whose name was Hiskil, and of his palace, but continued his journey to a small hut situated near the fence of the palace. Hiskil followed the king, racing his horse after him, when he real-ized that the king had come to his palace but would not enter it. The king saw the merchant, but he or-dered his guards not to let anybody to come near. When he arrived at the hut, a beautiful woman in the bloom of her years came out. Her name was Zabiba.

An aged man stood next to her, and it ap-peared that he was from her family. Zabiba greeted the king and reverently invited him to get off his horse and accept their hospitality.

The king dismounted his horse.

Zabiba invited the king to come in, and when the king entered the hut, she offered him a chair made out of bamboo stems. The king noticed that the hut was clean, and all things in it were in order and harmony.

*Did not the soul of the one who had sur-
rounded himself with a multitude of useless things
become burdened by the intricate maze of his palaces, their furniture and thick walls? Had not his
soul died as a result, having completely lost its aes-
thetic sense?*

*Does not an intimate connection to nature give
us the taste and ability to choose fitting colors, in the
same way that fresh air gives health to one's body
and peace to one's soul?*

Zabiba answered all the questions of the king
about her life and the king was amazed at the way
she spoke, and listened to her without interrupting.
Every time she addressed the king or answered his
questions, she spoke with dignity and respect, explaining herself simply and clearly, so that her
words calmed his soul and increased his knowledge.

The king was greatly impressed by Zabiba.

*Was not the simplicity of Zabiba, her natural
intelligence and lack of even the slightest pretense
the very thing this prisoner of the palace needed so
badly? He who heard and saw nothing apart from
what was long before predicted by the dull and boring pattern of his life?*

*But let us go back to what the old woman
was saying about the king; that is the very story on
which our narrative is based.*

After the king started frequently visiting the
house of Zabiba and after she started visiting him
at his palace and because of something that we
shall hear later, it happened that the king fell in
love with Zabiba and that with great passion, in
such a way as he had not loved any of his wives or
concubines. When she walked, his heart was ready
to burst out of his chest to catch up with her, fall
before her, and fly after her in order to find out

where she was going and to serve as a bright lantern for her.

But the king did not tell Zabiba of his love for her and tried to hide his attachment to her because he considered her one of the people and because his life was confined by the palace walls.

The king did not ask her about her husband and did not feel jealous of him because the husband had a legal right to her. However, the king was jealous of the air and the water and even of every morsel of food in her mouth. Yes, indeed, the king felt jealousy even about the mouth of Zabiba.

*Is it not the mouth that attracts a man to a woman or repels him from her? Does not a clever woman use her mouth to seduce a man, to attract him, and keep him? Does she not shade the imperfections of her mouth to insure that once a man comes close to it he will not distance himself?*

*Do not men kiss the lips of a woman more than any of her other beauties? Is the mouth not sufficient for some men to judge a woman's purity and prudence? And in any stage of their intimacy does not he cling to her mouth to prove his love to his beloved through kisses, which can be considered a sign of feelings independently of whether or not the couple had a sexual relationship? Is this not true? And if the meaning of the mouth is that great, should not a man be jealous about the mouth of the one he loves, her laughter, every movement of her lips? Clearly, one understands then why our mothers and grandmothers cover their mouths in front of strangers and why they only eat in the presence of their family. Clearly, one understands the meaning of the sacred verse which commands that women are to cover their open parts, and naturally, the mouth is among them.*

\*\*\*

The king loved Zabiba greatly. (And this story will tell you how much he loved her.)

The great king ordered his guards to let her into his private quarters, but did not describe his guest. The head of the guards was surprised that the news of the coming guest came directly from the king himself, but decided not to ask more and did not betray his doubts. He gathered the guards of the main gate and told them to put on their festive uniforms in preparation for meeting the king's guest.

"Let two guards open both parts of the gate," he instructed them. "Pull both doors inside simultaneously, so that neither door moves faster than the other." He also told them that the name of the king's guest was Zabiba.

When he mentioned the name of Zabiba, it did not tell them anything about her and did not at all seem to be familiar to them.

One of the guards nearly burst out laughing when he heard her name, but he limited himself to a smile when he saw the back of the chief's head in front of him.

After the chief of the guards left, the guards decided to entertain themselves with this conversation. One of them said:

"I would not mind having some raisins* today."

A second guard asked him, "Where will we get you raisins?"

Then another one said, "Doesn't a man always want what he cannot have?"

---

* *EDITOR'S NOTE:* Zabiba - means "a raisin" (singular) in Arabic.

And yet another added, "Is it shameful, my brother, to dream in one's imagination something that one cannot have?"

Then the previous asked, "Why torture your soul with what you cannot have? It is only a torment."

His friend answered, "A man's soul cannot exist in a way that he will demand of it, that is, without hope that it will reach beyond the limits of the possible."

Then the previous guard replied, "If hope is a state of power, as you suggest, which is inside of a man prior to his acting to make that hope a reality, then is not your hope in this case and a dream equally torturous? Because are we not destined to reside within the palace walls to guard it till they discharge us from the service, even though we see that people do not like those who live here, and therefore probably do not like us either?"

"But aren't we glad that we serve in the king's guard and can stuff our bellies with what is given to us while others are dying of hunger and get sick because of the lack of nourishment?"

"Yes, but aren't you tired of stuffing your gut while your soul is tortured with anxiety and lack of joy, when your brain is in disarray and your conscience suffers from premonitions?"

The oldest of them interrupted their conversation and said, "Truly, our friend's wish to have raisins *is* a torturous dream, because the one you are speaking about is the *king's* guest. Though it is clear from her name that the king will not be interested in her and will not give a banquet in her honor, it is likely that she is one of many, or otherwise I do not know how this grace was bestowed upon her. I do not know why the king wanted to see her because, mark my word, he'll reject her. And after all, she is just a single raisin. And what good will one raisin do for you? If she were a whole bag of raisins, then there would be at least some element of sense in your desire. So, why don't you quit dreaming and get about your duties?" He laughed and all the rest started laughing with him.

When they all settled down and one of the guards was marching back and forth by the gates, he heard footsteps. The guard looked intently into the dark and distinguished the silhouette of somebody approaching. He grasped his bow, took an arrow from the quiver, woke the other guards, and shouted to the approaching figure, "Stop, where you are!"

Zabiba uttered in a quivering, nervous voice, stuttering from fear, "Please, don't shoot! I am Z-Zabiba, the king's guest."

The guard came up to her and, very surprised, said, "Zabiba? The king's guest?"

"Yes," she said and shook her head to add certainty to her answer.

"Do come in, do come in," the guard said. "Forgive me, my lady, we did not recognize you. We imagined that you..."

"What was it that you imagined about me?"

The guard's respect helped her gain her confidence back, and now she spoke clearly again.

Before the guard had the time to answer, she said, "So, tell me, what is it that you imagined me to be like? Your expectations were false and you were doubly wrong when you thought that I was an unwelcome guest, trying to get into the palace in order to harm the one living in it. You thought that I would come in an entourage of carriages, with other carriages before and after mine? Does it not seem to you at all possible that a woman from common people, not unlike yourself, would be welcome in this palace? Am I not correct?"

"Yes, my lady," the guards replied.

And the oldest among them said, "Pardon us, my lady, but as part of our job what we imagine and expect is at least partially a reality. It is a part of what is possible and probable in the mind of the one imagining, and probability is not far off from reality and therefore is possible. How could you expect us to imagine that somebody from the common folk would be under the king's blessing and would be invited to meet with him, since that kind of thing had never happened before?"

Then Zabiba added to his words with a smile, "Especially if her name is Zabiba?"

"Yes, my lady."

He and the other guards would have smiled as well if they had not remembered that she was the king's guest and if the law and tradition had not forbidden the guards to smile in the presence of the king or his guests.

While Zabiba continued to joke with them, she asked with a slight laugh, "Do you know why I was called Zabiba?"

"No, my lady, please tell us," responded the guards merrily.

And she shared with them the story. "When my mother was carrying me, my family worked for the owner of a large property which had been granted to him by the father or grandfather of our king. The reason for the gift is unknown to me, and I could not find out anything about it, even though I've tried. But what is the reason why kings cut a portion of their country to give away to the important men? Is it not to either grant it as a prize, to cover their gambling debts, or to abandon it to the conquerors who have won victory over them?"

And though the guards were tough people themselves, they were amazed at the courage of Zabiba and at what she was implying. And because of her words, some of them smiled and some were silent, not showing their feelings. Isn't it from words like these that revolts start, luring people's souls after them? These words sow seeds of rebellion which spring up when the plan of resistance ripens, attracting the attention of all who feel the same way, prompting them to move in the same direction.

Zabiba continued, "My mother felt capricious and craved for raisins, but since neither she nor my father had any way of fulfilling that wish, she said to herself, 'I would be satisfied with just *one raisin.*'"

"Clearly, even that wish of hers could not be fulfilled. So, when she gave me birth she called me Raisin, *(for a woman has the right to name a female child herself).* That way she fulfilled her dream through my name, since she could not get even a single raisin when she wanted raisins so badly. She fulfilled her wish in me, and through that both her soul and her dream became immortal. She could not fulfill her wish after the grace of Allah came down upon her, for she died in giving me birth. And if she had not given me the name of Zabiba the king would not have chosen me, so that I could take pleasure in his love for me, or at least have the pleasure to be admired by him. And do you know why?"

And before the guards had answered her, she said, "Because the usual place for raisins is in the storehouses of the rich and the merchants, on the tables of kings and important courtiers. But when I have an opportunity, I will make sure that even you can taste raisins and even nuts. Who knows?"

Zabiba said that with a merry smile and all of her beauty came back to her. Even though her dress was simple, it was kept clean, and the hair on her head was in order, slightly covered with a scarf.

Then the chief of the guards, walking towards them in a stately manner, screamed at them,

"Why have you gathered here? Go back to your places, now!"

The older guard said to him, "My lord, this is the king's guest, the lady Zabiba."

"What?"

"Yes, my lord, I am Zabiba, the king's guest."

Only now did the head of guards notice the woman standing among them. Then he asked, "Is what she says true?"

Then he came up to her and asked with surprise, "You are Zabiba?"

"Yes, my lord, I am Zabiba, the king's guest. Didn't the king inform you that I will be his guest tonight?" She spoke firmly, as if to spite the chief of the guards, with a confident voice, carrying a kind of strength that comes from pride and self assurance, for she *was* the king's guest.

The head of the guards said, "Forgive me, but..."

"What, dear chief of the guard? Or perhaps I, one of the people, am not fit to be his guest? Or perhaps you have the power to alter the king's decision?"

"Oh, no, not me, nor could any other ever alter king's decision and his will! Forgive me, lady Zabiba, but we did not think that any of the king's guests and especially those that come to him at night could be a common man or a woman. At times, during large festivities, the king would present himself before the common people, to see how the people greet him from afar, but *never* have we seen what we see before our eyes right now."

Then the feeling of pride for being the only such recipient of the king's grace intoxicated her, and she said, "Then let me be the first. Is it really that unusual, that among those who sit with the king and among those who serve him or perhaps among his concubines there will be a common woman?"

"Don't the noble lords from the rich merchants and important generals, ministers and emirs have absolute control over the time and kingdom of the king? Let them keep their riches and the kingdom, but let them leave the king for us."

Zabiba smiled and turned her question to the guards, who listened to her with great attention, "Isn't what I am saying just?"

And all replied to her, "Yes, my lady, it is just."

The chief, having glanced sternly at the guards, who were agreeing with Zabiba when they were supposed to be silent, said, "Pardon me, my lady, I have to report your arrival to the main hadjib.*

It became clear to Zabiba that until that moment the chief of the guards was not sure whether she really was the guest of the king of whom he had previously been told, and he could not believe her completely.

And Zabiba said, "Do what your duty commands you."

And when the chief of the guards left, Zabiba said to herself, "Isn't faithfulness and doing one's duty the responsibility of each one of us? Therefore, I should not be angry with the chief of the guards because, according to his duty, he has to make sure that what I say is really true and that I am not an impostor. He should question to be sure I am the king's guest and not somebody else and that my name really belongs to me, because it is not from the list of the names that the chief is accustomed to

---

* *EDITOR'S NOTE:* Hadjib – means literally "door-keeper," an official in the palace hierarchy.

among those people that he is used to dealing with."

The chief of the guards came back in a hurry. "Forgive me, my lady! I beg your mercy," he said, and added many more flattering and ingratiating words, interrupting them with frequent bows, so that she would be pleased by him.

Zabiba knew the cause for this, because she supposed that the main hadjib must have shouted at him and scolded him for the delay. Or possibly that the king himself had done that. And what if the king were rude when dealing with people?

She asked herself, "What if it was the king himself who dealt harshly with him?"

Then she answered, "Probably the king was not among those who did it. For isn't it true that those who surround the king are exceedingly more cruel that the king himself? The ministers must have punished the chief. The king wouldn't do it."

And then, still to herself, she added "Didn't the head of the guards act according his duty? What if things were the other way around? What if he did not make sure who I was and led me before the king, but I wasn't the person the king invited? What would have happened to him then? Doesn't the one who is further away from the king have more freedom?"

And she answered, "Perhaps the one who is further away from the king has more freedom, but that does not satisfy me. This is my opportunity, and it would be stupid to let it slip away, especially since it concerns the king himself. For this king is our king. To be far from him means to have no active resources for life, because to be far from the king means to be far from power and property, whether it be personal or property of the state. The one who has no access to property is defenseless before life, nature and its creatures, and the one who is defenseless can be easily overcome by nature and its creatures. He will be either forced into an exile or torn into pieces. The one who is torn into pieces will lose his freedom when he dies, because his death is not the fight that life demands from him; he has made a foolish choice in his dealings in life. And the one who shall be forced into exile will also lose his freedom. Nature and its creatures will overcome the madman. The essence of the supremacy of the human mind is in his ability to invent and find resources which would allow him to overpower living things and to adjust to nature. A man cannot do that if he does not acquire these resources, and property is foremost among these resources, whether it belongs to all people together or to any one person in particular. By means of such symbols as the state and the things it possesses, a man, his mind, and other human qualities reach the necessary supremacy, depending upon different conditions and circumstances. If we desire freedom, we should not allow those in power to possess everything they want, because by that we deprive ourselves of freedom. And if we allow that, any talk about freedom and equality will be empty chatter. If everyone from the start had everything they needed in equal share, and if everyone would give back what would be considered excessive for a man, then who would desire freedom or chase what is called freedom? But since all of that is not so, even when people start a marathon from the same line, some of them run faster and some slower. The results of their *abilities* are not equal. Does not the fact that we achieve different results in that marathon independently of our wishes and intentions, explain the differences in the resources we possess?"

So said Zabiba to herself as she and the chief of the guards reached the quarters of the main guard, who took Zabiba to the inner gates of the king's palace.

Having entered the gates with the main guard, Zabiba started examining all the details of the palace corridor. She was about to walk into where the king was waiting for her in the middle of the corridor, but noticed that the main guard suddenly stopped, saluted with a loud stomp and froze.

The king said to him, "Thank you, you can leave Zabiba now and go."

The guard turned around in a similarly trained manner and left them alone.

Zabiba greeted the king and, slightly bending her knees and holding the folds of her dress, bowed her head so that she looked like a butterfly. She looked beautiful even though her dress was not really appropriate for the palace and did not look like the dresses of the princesses, wives and daughters of the rich, which are appropriate to wear in the palace during the festivities, both big and small. It did not even look like a dress of a concubine.

The king smiled, greeting his guest, "Welcome, welcome to the palace!"

He took two steps toward her so that he could touch her, slightly lifted her head, then hugged her, and said, "I missed you, my dear."

It alarmed Zabiba that the king called her "dear" and she turned the word around in her mind, saying to herself, "Does the king really find me dear to his heart or is he just saying it to flatter me? But why and in what manner did he find me dear? He is used to seeing very special women, not at all like me. They are from the court of women and the daughters of his ministers and emirs, and they are so many."

"Excuse me, my lord the king, but why and in what manner do you find me dear?"

"You certainly deserve to be called dear, Zabiba. As soon as I met you, this word was firmly planted in my soul; since the time when I came to your house and returned again and again when you were on the land of the one who bothered us and whom we chased off of the land which had been granted to him by a previous king."

The king recalled that one of his royal predecessors had granted to his minister a large portion of land, where he became a tradesman and started raising different animals and plants. He put up some beehives and started selling honey. Then that man started trading all over the kingdom and beyond, and his possessions were worth an enormous number of shekels.*

And every time when that tradesman would encounter the king, he told him how wonderful and delicious his honey was, better than any honey on the market and even better than the honey that the king's servants collected far from the lands and gardens of the king. So it was, until the day the king sent one of his courtiers to buy a large quantity of this honey for the palace. When those who knew something about good honey tried some of it, it turned out that the honey was fake. The fraud was as following: the greedy tradesman emptied the combs, taking the honey away from the bees, so that nothing was left. Instead of honey, he put something else in the hives for the bees to eat during winter. As a result of this, the taste of the honey changed and lost its natural qualities, becoming very different from the honey of other bees. That is

---

* *A FOOTNOTE OF THE ORIGINAL AUTHOR:* "Originally, the shekel was a measure for silver and gold. This measure was used by Akkadians, Babylonians and Assyrians, and in the era of Assyrian rule it was used as currency. After the first and second exile of the Judeans by Nebuchadnezzar in 589 and 587 BCE, the Jews adopted that measure from the Babylonians and made it their own."

why the king took the land back from that swindler and made it state property again.

At that time, Zabiba's father worked on the estate of this tradesman, and when the property was restored to the state, the king left those workers and farmers who wanted to stay on the land. Zabiba's father was among them. Zabiba soon got married. And when the king happened to be on that land, he saw Zabiba and she caught his attention, but he also caught her fancy. The king became a frequent visitor on that land and fell in love with Zabiba, while she fell in love with him.

And the king said, "When I called you dear, it was not an empty expression, but a reflection of the form and substance which you combine in yourself."

"But there are women who are much more beautiful than I, and I have seen many of them. Forgive me for speaking openly and perhaps with indiscretion, but you probably have even had many of them, too."

"But I have never met among them a single one who would be as dear in heart, soul, beauty, and character as you are, Zabiba!"

"How could that be, O great king!"

"Almost all of them tried to get close to the king in hope for his crown or power and not for any other reason, but the crown is not at all more important than my personal qualities, Zabiba."

"But could one actually separate form from substance, my king? You said that I am dear and gave me reasons for calling me so, among them mentioning my form as beautiful. Isn't the crown also a part of your form?"

"The crown is a part of my external appearance, but it is not my form as a whole. Besides I do not think that form for a man is as important as it is in a woman. The crown is a thing, Zabiba. Could you really judge the worth of the king by the things he possesses?"

"No, Your Majesty. To judge a person correctly, one must judge his substance, qualities, and character as a whole. A form, however, should be judged just as a bonus to the other characteristics. The person for whom things become a defining criteria will judge not the man himself but his things. The person who evaluates a man by examining the things around him sees in that man only a thing to be used and does not see in him the human traits on which one could rely. Personally, I cannot imagine a man as a mere thing, even in the case of that contemptible individual whom you drove away from the land and whose property you confiscated."

"I would like to talk about a specific person—the king, not about general philosophical notions."

"General notions fit this situation because they are related to a human being. Let us not forget about that aspect."

The king replied nothing to these words but said, "You said, Zabiba, that you could not imagine that contemptible tradesman whom we drove off the land as a mere thing, didn't you?"

"Yes, Your Majesty."

"Do you mean that he has no value at all? Or if he has, is it so miserable that he could not even be called a thing?"

"No, my great king, I did not mean that. This is what I wanted to say. Even in light of the fact that he is contemptible and your decision is right, still we cannot think of him as a thing, for he is a descendent of Adam, though it is possible that he has lost his humanity or that it has become very weak within him. But in every son of Adam, no matter how miserable of a person he might be, will remain a particle of humanity, even if evil permeates his qualities and character, so that he looks like a thing."

The king said, "But can you extract that small measure of positive qualities from all the evil qualities that permeate him, Zabiba?"

"Reformers would try to do that, Your Majesty," answered Zabiba. "They would be able to cultivate in him that small measure of positive qualities so that it became predominant in his character, while all the bad departed and disappeared."

"But the king is not a social reformer, Zabiba."

"Oh, if only a ruler would also become a social reformer besides being a source of many other decisions. Then everything could be different," said Zabiba.

"A man cannot accomplish everything he wants," answered the king.

"But couldn't he appoint somebody else to do it? So that that person would not have to be distracted by issues of power and would not be a segment of the governmental chain of authority? So that the government had no responsibility for the things that person would be doing?"

"There is nothing that is impossible, Zabiba."

"I had never thought of that before. And what about you, my great king, have you ever thought of yourself as a part of a people's council?"

"I thought that peoples' councils obeyed the state, Zabiba."

"A people's council which is good for the state, my great king, appoints the government; government does not appoint the council. And if the king were a part of the council, wouldn't the council merely obey the wishes of the king? You could easily make it so that the people's council, as I described it, would take upon itself immediate leadership over the people and would try to fix what can be fixed, while you and those who support you could assume power according to the hierarchy."

"But right now, I and those who support me have power even without that council. And that means that the government is not appointed and that the reality of power precedes the idea of a peoples' council. However, I have come to the conclusion that we need some type of an organization to lead a reform. If you prefer to call it the 'people's council,' Zabiba, may it be so."

"Traditional power is capable of creating the people's council of which you spoke. But do you actually want the people's council to remain a mere formality or a veil to cover the defects of the existing government? Or do you want this people's council to build up society as a whole and actually accomplish reform?"

"I rather prefer the second variant, but let us be realistic."

"What do you mean by 'realistic,' my great king? Only the things to which we try to adjust and attempt to fit into the existing system, or what we are capable of creating by transforming the character of power and resources, and thereby changing the very notion of reality?"

"I mean what you said last, Zabiba. But I also want to say that the task of forming a people's council that will produce radical changes in society, push it forward, and bring it to the next level is not a task fitting for the government, but the task of revolutionaries and fighters. Then the government will give birth to it, not the other way around. Its goals would be the goals of the people, and that council will exist for the purpose of reform."

"I think that it is not impossible to form a people's council even under the current government. It would have some, but not all of the elements of a revolutionary council in a traditional setting. In this case, it would be capable of changing some areas of the people's life for the better, but not everything that needs to be changed."

"What do you mean, Zabiba?"

"When you form a people's council and you are a part of it, make the council a part of the people and do not rely on those who have significant influence, high position, or great wealth, but rely on the common people. Make it so that the basis of it is made out of the least prosperous people. But you will not be able to do all of this unless you yourself become one with the people."

"But how can I become one with the people, Zabiba, when in reality I am their king?"

"You have to become a part of the people with all your soul and conscience, with all your life and thoughts. You need to place a high goal of achievement before the people and the people's council, a goal which corresponds to the meaning of our state and its role in the life and mission of its citizens. You need to lead the people and the people's council to that goal honestly and wholeheartedly, without forcing them to compromise their principles. You need to gather all those who are pure in their deeds and thoughts, and you yourself need to do what you exhort your people and the people's council to do. You need to be honest and just from the very beginning and to the very end."

"But is what you are saying, Zabiba. . . is that easy to do?"

"No, it is difficult, my king, but for the very reason that it is hard to do, your success will be firmly established. No wind of change will destroy it, as happens with those achievements which are easily done. What is easy to do people usually do not accept. That is why an easily achieved goal leaves as easily as it appeared, allowing something new to take its place."

"You are right, Zabiba. We should continue this discussion to figure out what is actually better, but we must do it some other time."

"As you wish, my king."

"But before we close the door of discussion, I wanted to express one concern. What if a conflict occurs between those in the people's council and those in power? What if the members of the people's council start competing with those in power for our privileges instead of taking care of doing what is beneficial for the people and the state?"

"It could happen, my king, if everything else remains the way it is right now. That is, if you simply add to the already existing governmental offices one more name: the people's council. But if everything goes according to the plan that we have been discussing just now; if you place some patriotic goals before the people's council corresponding to the high goals which are beneficial for the people to achieve; if the people's council comes into the arena of life where it has an opportunity for risk and self sacrifice, then it will have earned the right to organize the people, and it will do so without further enforcement. In that case, you can appoint all the duties so that each member has his own responsibility and so that there are no confrontations and competition between members of the people's council and the representatives of the government. But from a practical point of view, I think that at any time, on any level, and under any conditions, absolute separation of these entities is impossible."

The corridor through which they were walking was long and dusky, because the candles along the walls were not bright enough to light the way to the chambers of the king.

Zabiba said, "Do you notice, my king, that this corridor, and actually the whole palace, seems to be abandoned and desolate?"

"It may seem so because there are no windows in the corridors and in some rooms of the palace. Or it may be because it is your first time here. You haven't been to the king's palace before, have you?" asked the king with a smile.

"The fact that this is my first time in the king's palace is true, and I thank our Creator for the opportunity to meet you and to benefit from your kindness and graciousness. But this is not my first time in a palace. I have been in the palace of Hiskil, the landowner whom you made leave; and his palace is much like yours, as you know. They say that the master wanted to marry the young concubines of your father after his death, because he wanted to look like a king and fancied to conquer the throne if he had a palace like that of a king and wives from those who used to be the king's concubines," said Zabiba with loud laughter.

Then she turned to the king with a bow and uttered, "Forgive me, great king, it is not I, but my soul which laughed at the fact that there are such people, who have many possessions and yet have base souls."

"How is it that you say that your soul was laughing and not you yourself?"

"My king, if you were to command me to make a choice, I would not laugh in your presence. But my soul, which is not used to the palace etiquette, jumped beyond the limits of the appropriate and laughed."

"Very well, Zabiba, but why would you force your soul to do the things that are contrary to it? I would like it if you gave your soul more freedom to be natural."

"But does a common woman like me need freedom?" said Zabiba, as if it were not she who said it, but her very soul.

27

The king started laughing, and she, intoxicated with a very strange feeling, added, "A king is laughing with a common woman?"

"I am the king of a great country. I love when the people are free and I love to express myself sometimes by having a good laugh with the common folk, though I don't want to do that all the time."

Zabiba said, "Yes, great king. If you speak naturally with the common people, they come back to their human state, but if you treat them as if they were puppets, they could rebel."

Then she added, "But if you wish you could laugh with the common folk, why do you stay here locked up in your palace?"

"Am I really locked up, Zabiba? The guards that you saw when you entered are here to protect me, not to keep me under guard. They are a part of my royal majesty."

"They are surrounding you, those guards. They are keeping you in and they are guarding those locked doors and empty corridors. They guard this empty palace where I have yet to notice any movement except for the movement of your seeking soul, your majesty. All this, in fact, limits you. Your guards and your servants, without even realizing it, limit you. For you, my king, sit here under house arrest, even though nobody ordered you to it. How could one say they love freedom and build a palace without windows which let in light and air? How could one love nature and wish that I would behave according to my nature and yet have no direct connection to nature and not even be able to enjoy its beauty through the windows?"

"Calm down, Zabiba. I will explain everything to you. There are not many windows in the palace for security reasons. If you make too many windows in the palace, the guards will have a harder time protecting it."

"But it makes the palace so desolate, my king. Isn't loneliness the worst enemy of one in power? And to put an end to this loneliness, one must flee it. Leave the loneliness of the palace, my king, and let your soul do what is natural for it. Come out to nature and the people. Are not nature and the people the best cure for the loneliness in your soul?"

"I used to do what you say, Zabiba, or at least almost what you describe, when I first entered the palace, but then I discovered that the courtiers found my behavior to be strange and rebuked me. Probably they thought that my making changes to the traditions of the palace was caused by frivolity and ignorance of what is appropriate. In the end, I had to accept the traditions. Wouldn't a person who has lived in a palace for seven years have already developed some habits?"

"Of course, my king," answered Zabiba. "A habit is permissible, even if it is bad, provided one does not ignore its root cause. That is why one must be very careful to distinguish what is permissible for him to do and what is not. You are used to this palace because you did not reject a habit and have sacrificed that which was natural, for the sake of your position and self-assurance. As for me, I am not used to the palace yet, for I do not want to accept it, and I am sure that I do not accept what it stands for. Why does anyone accept the principles of confinement, which are required for one to accept, especially if there is a choice?"

"A choice of what, Zabiba?"

"A choice for you to leave the palace and to find yourself among people with whom you can live and whose resources you can share. Look, my great king, at how thick are the walls of this palace where you live. It has no windows which would allow you to see and hear the things that happen beyond these walls. The halls of this palace are arranged so that you cannot even see the other people who are in the palace."

"Any means are justified if they achieve the goals dictated by the interests of power and security, Zabiba."

"Truly, all that I see and much of what I hear from you, my king, appears to be a burden to you rather than a prompting for you to take action and resolve the governmental tasks with the means that the king and his people have their disposal. Truly, your palace is a den for breeding demons, my king! That is because demons come out of forsaken palaces, and your palace is desolate. Its walls are thick and its windows are few. The palace is gloomy; the air smells of rot; movements are limited and monotonous. It looks like a place which Shaitan* himself chose to breed and do his evil deeds. And where Shaitan dwells, you can be sure betrayal is being plotted. There, jealousy and greed brew, and there, thirst for power grows strong. The walls of the palace do not allow you to see light or to breath fresh air. They will mute even your own voice when traitors should attack you, and no one will hear you outside or come to rescue you. The palace will trap you when they try to overpower you. The dark corners will help your enemies to hide their khinjars* and arrows intended for you, my king."

"Yes, Zabiba, your words are true and just, but do you really want me to resign from the throne and live away from the palace, as I used to live forgotten by my father, may Allah be merciful to him,

---

* **EDITOR'S NOTE:** Shaitan – means Satan, or Devil in Muslim usage.
* **EDITOR'S NOTE:** Khinjar - a short, slightly curved sword.

because of the plotting of the brothers and sons of his concubines?"

At that time, they finally reached the king's chambers. After a short pause, Zabiba said to the king, "Forgive me, my great king, do you mind if we continue our conversation?"

"No, not at all. Please, say whatever you wish, Zabiba."

"You asked me, much surprised, whether I wanted you to actually live away from the palace, as you used to live forgotten by your father, the previous king, may Allah be merciful to him, which, as you said, happened because of the plotting of the brothers and sons of his concubines. Before I answer you, my king, would you be so kind to tell me. . . . I would like to hear that story. You said that you grew up alone away from the capitol and not in the palace like your brothers and other emirs.** Did I hear you correctly?"

"Yes, Zabiba."

"So, please, I beg you, my king, forgive my persistence, tell me this story before I respond to your question. I beg you to do so, because if you satisfy this wish of mine it will help me to be free in my spirit. Also, it will fill my mind and soul with what is needed to answer to your question well. That is my wish. Give me at least a short moment when I feel like an equal, even in a simple human sense, and I will give you comfort. But without that feeling, my king, if you just play a theatrical role, I will not be able to keep my soul calm, and won't be

---

** **EDITOR'S NOTE:** Emir translated from Arabic means "prince," that is a son of the reigning king, who had claims to the throne. Due to the large size of the harems of legal wives and concubines that belonged to eastern rulers many descendants aspired to the kingship.

able to be of any real help to you in personal matters."

"Zabiba, you should go back to your family now so that I can go back to my business. I will tell you all that next time."

Zabiba said, "If you so wish, my king. When do you command for me to come again?"

The king answered, "I do not command you, Zabiba. I only express my wishes."

"Isn't the wish of a king the law, my great king?"

"In that case, I 'suggest' rather than wish, if you like that choice of words better, Zabiba."

"I wouldn't mind it even if your desire came in a form of command, because most important is not the form but the substance. Because I have seen your substance through our conversations, I will not allot any significance merely to the form. So, when do you want me to come, my king? Today is Monday. Is Friday a good day? Oh, but forgive me, king, Friday is the day of worship, when we pray to Allah, as is our tradition."

"In that case, come on Saturday, if Saturday is good for you, Zabiba."

"Yes, my great king, doubly do I thank you. Firstly for deciding to continue a relationship with me, and for not forgetting me right away, and secondly, for respecting my religious beliefs. Saturday is good."

She said good-bye to the king and left.

When Zabiba came out of the palace, she saw that a horse-keeper was waiting for her at the door, and near him was a gray mare.

The horse-keeper said to her, "This is a gift from the king, my lady."

"But how shall I feed her? And who will take care of it?" thought Zabiba.

And before she could say anything, the had-jib came up to her and put a pouch of gold into the saddlebag. Then Zabiba said, "Though the people curse kings, kings certainly know something about generosity that the people do not."

She said these words to herself and shivered, feeling a pang of conscience. Then she thought, "Is such generosity common for kings and is it really their proper quality? Yet is not the sacrificial generosity of the people the best kind of generosity? For a man from among the people kills the bull with which he cultivates the land and on which his very existence depends, for the king when he comes to visit. He gives the food which he prepared for his children to a stranger to whom he extended his hospitality, and leaves his own children hungry. Unlike the poor man, does the wealth of a king diminish if he gives away a small portion of it? Isn't the common man more noble than the king?"

She saddled the horse and headed home.

***

Zabiba returned to the king's palace as they had planned.

And while she was walking down the corridors of the palace, in anticipation of the meeting, she saw that the ladies of the queen were gathering at the entrances of the corridors leading toward the main gallery, whispering and giggling. But when she came closer, they greeted her respectfully and perhaps even with certain friendliness, which they tried to hide. Zabiba noticed that by their eyes. The eyes do not lie, and an experienced person can always read what is written in a person's glance; at least, whether the eyes speak of love or hate.

Suddenly, a woman appeared in the gallery. Her dress signified her greatness, yet the way she walked and the way she related to her courtiers and maids did not increase her respectability or grace. She was tall, and the lines of her body were amazing. She was rather slim, but not without feminine flesh, gentle and igniting desire in men. Everything about her appearance was beautiful, but Zabiba could not judge her soul, her heart, and the kind of qualities for which the queen herself could be held responsible. She could not be held responsible for her external appearance and the peculiarities of her body, all of which she had from her birth. As for the qualities such as morality, taste, manners, politeness, culture, education, and such, for these a person is responsible, at least in some measure. It is upon these that the level of success or failure in the matters of marital relations and love depend. On them the relationship between the husband and wife is built, and on them love in all its variety and in all stages is sustained. That is why so much is revealed immediately after the engagement, first wedding night, or first pregnancy, when a man and a woman finally realize what was most important for them when they made the choice, when they decided to join in a union.

But how can one find a balance between form and spirit? How does one know if he gives preference to the form only or if his choice was shaped by the things ideal and spiritual?

The woman did not wish Zabiba good evening, nor did she wait for Zabiba to greet her, but hardly containing herself, asked sternly, "Are you Zabiba?"

Zabiba replied, "Good evening, my lady."

Then she continued, full of self confidence, but without arrogance or challenge, "Yes, I am Zabiba, the daughter of the people, and I am fortunate to be loved by my lord, my king."

"Do you know who I am?" The queen asked.

"Forgive me, my lady. Please, do not take offense at my words, if I don't take a guess. My guess may be erroneous or imprecise, and I dare not make a mistake since I have not had the honor of being introduced to you before."

"Does my appearance tell you nothing?"

"Forgive me, my lady, but external appearance does not always reveal one's substance. In any case, it never gives a complete idea of what one might be. That is why when you saw me, you asked me whether or not I was Zabiba. If it were enough for you just to look at me once to tell who I was, it would be enough for me and I would tell you right away without asking any questions. So that is why I tell you that I am Zabiba, the daughter of my people, who is fortunate to be loved by his majesty the king."

"You are a common woman. I could tell that simply by looking at you," said the queen, trying to ridicule Zabiba's appearance, in which she looked like neither a princess nor a queen. "But one wouldn't even guess that you are the king's concubine from your looks either."

Zabiba replied, "I am the daughter of my people, and that quality, having encompassed both my appearance and my substance, became my clear and definite quality. That is why I am proud of it. The customs and traditions which the people do not respect are not genuine. Though I am fortunate and proud to be loved by the king, the traditions and appearances that the people do not embrace cannot appeal to me. I have retained my substance and my external appearance, and combining these qualities I can offer my service to the ideas and traditions of the people, instead of adding my persona to the number of courtiers burdened by their heavy chains."

"Why do you say the courtiers are chained, daughter of the people?" the queen demanded in an insulting tone.

Zabiba answered, "I do not mean all, but only some of them. But no one put chains on them. They did it themselves, trying to adjust to the things that are wrong. That is why those who preferred chains are now chained, but those who did not want them are free, even though they did not leave the palace. Isn't freedom as well as status indicated by how one feels inside, my lady?"

When Zabiba said that, she saw that many among the servants and ladies in waiting who were listening to their conversation would have been ready to applaud, if it were not happening in the palace, and if it were not the queen who was standing before her.

The queen noticed this as well and raised her voice. "Enough of this philosophical talk. Speak in a language that we can all understand!"

Zabiba said, "Forgive me, my queen, but I am not trained to speak eloquently in your language. I am the daughter of my people, as you have noticed, and as I, myself, have previously mentioned there is no hope for me to start speaking in your language." Her words held several meanings for those in the culture of that region of the Euphrates.

The queen, losing her temper, screamed at the courtiers and palace maids who were listening to their conversation, "What are you standing here for? Go! Go away! Leave us alone! Leave me with Zabiba alone!"

One of the most influential ladies asked the queen with surprise, "Should I leave also, my lady?"

"Yes, you too."

The same question came from the hadjib, who received a similar answer. No one was left but the queen and Zabiba, while the others crowded

36

behind the doors, trying their hardest to overhear their conversation. They continued talking, walking back and forth down the main corridor of the king's palace.

The queen asked Zabiba, "Why do you keep the king to yourself and force him to distance himself from the rest of us, Zabiba?"

"Excuse me, my lady, but the king is free in his actions. Nobody is holding him."

"No, you claimed him for yourself without thinking about us."

"And again, you are mistaken, my lady. God forbid that I made a claim on the king, the ruler of the people and of our great kingdom."

"The main thing is that he is a king," the queen said. "He must give his attention to us. I should be his main concern, and then he can think of others."

Then Zabiba said to the queen, "That is why you have lost the king, my lady."

"What are you trying to say?" snapped the queen.

Zabiba replied, "Truly, selfishness along with unbridled desires seeking after personal gain, leads to a situation in which people, even a queen, are treated as if they were not human beings, but merely things. People are prone to think, feel, and understand what is good and what is bad and then choose what is best for them."

"And how is it that you are better than we, daughter of the people?"

"Forgive me, my lady, but I do not place myself higher than you or the other wives and concubines of the king and do not even try to be compared with you. However, we have met, he and I, and our views and feelings agreed, and something happened of which you know absolutely nothing."

"The king could never forget our relationship of many years just because you seduced him in your first meeting with him. He will not leave us to stay with you."

"No, my lady, not from the first meeting and not from the first glance did we fall in love. It happened over the time necessary for our feelings to coincide. And when they did, the result was inevitable."

"Tell me, Zabiba, how are you different from us?"

"Forgive me, queen, but I can't. I do not want to compare myself with anyone, because the one who speaks highly of herself is more likely to be lost rather than being on her way to her destination, more likely to be on the edge of a cliff than on a gradual slope."

The queen scrutinized Zabiba and said, "Look, are you taller than I? Are your eyes, waist, legs, neck, complexion, and... and... are they more beautiful than mine?"

The queen took a few steps away from Zabiba, then turned and said, "It must be that the people have planted roots into the soul of the king, and the king became bored with the queen's beauty, the daughters of other kings, and the nobility. He got tired of the concubines that other kings, emirs, and tradesmen of his kingdom and other lands gave to him. To all of them, he has preferred a common woman."

When Zabiba heard how the queen mocked her, she became angry, but controlling herself replied with these words: "Perhaps the king *is* tired of what is familiar and it does not arouse him any longer. Understanding of the common people, that is what he did not find in you and in those you mention. One who does not understand the common people and the laws of life does not know how to use her wealth, power, and high position. She does not know the friends of her husband. She does not know who serves him and who carries the banners of his kingdom."

She continued, "You have lost the connection with the people and you do not know the rules of this life, in which people who are good-natured, who have lively minds and sound thinking rather than just attractive externals, have the victory. The mercy of Allah who gave you this beautiful form did not prompt you to thank Allah for it with your deeds and thoughts, and that is why you cannot even manage your own beauty. A man may be attracted by beauty, especially if he is young, and therefore, may not find in his chosen a good nature, prudence, or taste. Still, soon after his first wedding night he will begin watching for influential and substantive qualities in her. If he finds none, he will continue his search in other places and in other women.

"My lady, ask the king himself what he was attracted to in me, and he will answer you better than I ever could. But since you are asking me what brought me so close to the king and about the character and the qualities that allowed for it, I can tell you what I know and what I suspect to be true."

The queen became furious and again snapped, "The king is no stranger to me and now that we have lived together for so many years, I know him completely in every way."

"Forgive me, my lady, do not take offense if I say that you don't know anything about the king which is not on the surface or what is not known by the others. And that is because you are not trying to know him or perhaps are not capable of seeing those parts of his mind and soul which are invisible to most. That is why you did not really get to know him in all these years that you have lived near him.

And because you did not know him, you never found out how to become close to him and influence him."

The queen replied as if trying to insult Zabiba, "How could anyone besides me be closer to the king if I am the one who shares his bed?" Having said that, she started laughing hysterically while all of her courtiers, maids, and servants started laughing with her, and someone even cracked the door open so that she could hear that they were laughing with her.

"Is appearance not the very thing that delights the eyes of the king?" she asked. It seemed that the queen did not care whether the courtiers were laughing at her or at Zabiba, as long as they were laughing, though it was clear that everyone was laughing *at* the queen's weak mind, and *with* Zabiba. But Zabiba herself was not laughing.

She answered the queen with these words: "No, my lady, the fact that you are sleeping in the same bed with the king does not make you closest to him. You would have been much closer if you were to enter his heart to the very depths of his soul. It is I who am in his heart right now, and you are left out, even though I am not sharing his bed. I took your place in his soul while you were just in his bed. That is why he chose me and has withdrawn from you."

Now Zabiba started laughing and all the doors leading into the hall where she and the queen were opened. Laughter was heard from all floors of the palace.

Then the queen screamed in rage, "Stop that, all of you! Curse you, curse Zabiba!"

And Zabiba replied calmly, "May the One and Only strengthen all of those whose hearts were not captured by the shaitan or led astray by him. And may he cover with shame the names of those who are dull, cruel, or stubborn."

Turning around without asking the queen for permission to leave, she departed, heading in the same direction in which she was going before being interrupted.

\*\*\*

The noise, voices, and laughter attracted the attention of the king's hadjib, who was in the adjoining chamber. He came out, took Zabiba by the hand, and escorted her to the room where the king was waiting for her. As was customary, he knocked on the door, entered, greeted the king, and left, so that Zabiba was left alone with the king.

After a while, Zabiba reminded the king of his promise to tell her the story of his youth and asked him reverently, "Please, do not be offended by my persistence, my great king, but I so much want to hear the story that you promised to tell me. Doesn't the one who loves long to know all about her beloved? You are my king and my beloved, so forgive my insistence, my master, and grant me my wish."

The king said, "I will tell you this story, Zabiba."

And the king began, "It was a long time ago. My father married my mother at the dawn of his youth and she was his cousin, born in our palace. She gave me birth after much suffering and my father rejoiced, may Allah be gracious to him. My mother told me about it. And my father stopped worrying about the future of his kingdom, because his son, a male, was to replace him on his throne, keeping it in the family line. My mother, the queen, had a very special relationship with my father and her role in the kingdom was unique. When the king was occupied with business away from the capitol, the queen herself managed things in the kingdom, but only to the extent that the king allowed her to, so that there would be no disagreement between the two of them. However after my mother gave birth to me, she could not conceive again, and the king started to worry about his kingdom once more. What could be done? What would happen if I were killed? So, he decided to take wives for himself from the women which he captured in raids and conquests. Perhaps it was even my mother herself who advised him to do so, having realized that the desire had already entered his heart. My mother thought that the new wives could not challenge her position by the virtue of their status, because she was the queen and they were merely concubines, mothers of his children. There even was a rumor that she chose the first one for him."

"But then their number grew larger, didn't it, my king?"

"Yes, Zabiba, he did take many more," answered the king. "But be patient, and you will find out everything in its time. My mother chose the first wife for the king without his participation. She was not very beautiful, while my mother was a real beauty and had an appearance worthy of royalty. Could a woman in that situation choose someone as beautiful as she or even someone who would dare to compete with her? My father married that concubine but without much desire, just for the sake of his wife, so that she did not feel jealous toward her and her happy life was not clouded. But my mother did not take into consideration the fact that external beauty is not always the defining factor. My father took that concubine for a wife and she bore a male baby for him, then a second one, and a third. So my father got what he wanted and calmed his worries over the possibility of something bad happening to me. After that, he took another wife for himself, and this time after his own choice, the most beautiful, most intelligent, and good-natured of his concubines. Does not the one who marries a second time leave behind his negative attitude toward polygamy? Doesn't the proverb say that the one whose clothes are wet isn't afraid of the rain? Because his conscience was now seared and with hopes of having as many sons as possible so that they would become swords around the heir to the throne, that would be me, my father continued to take more of his concubines for wives and continued to have more sons. Among all of his sons I was the only son of the queen. When my brothers grew up, my mother was not welcome among his wives, for when she was among them, or rather, in charge of them, they felt bitter because of the obvious difference in their position and influence. When the king and other important people paid attention to the queen, their chances to be noticed by others diminished. My mother, who was so distinct among them, was considered a stranger. Don't people feel jealous of those who have a special place? Don't the envious hate them? The slopes of the mountain may not always be proud of their peak. They groan under its weight and create earthquakes that could be fatal for the top," said the king and smiled at Zabiba, though it was obvious that he was deeply grieved.

From time to time, he sighed so deeply that it seemed as if he could not get enough air. And when a tear streamed down his cheek, Zabiba stopped it with the tips of her fingers and then placed them on her own cheek. She was determined not to cry with the king, so that he would not have to think of how to comfort her instead of grieving for his own pain which he was revealing. She wanted to hear everything to the end and then share her thoughts with him. At least, she wanted to tell him the things that she felt might be helpful for the king.

"The number of the king's wives and concubines grew larger. When he would tire of one of them, another would find his favor, and so they would constantly switch places, all fighting for a special place in their relationship with him.

"So they all united against my mother and my father, and under the influence of rumors, started to chip away at my mother's influence.

"Do kings not also believe more in what they hear than in what they see and feel?" thought Zabiba to herself, listening to the story about the king's father.

The king continued his narrative. "So, the day came when my mother fell mysteriously ill and died, may Allah be merciful to her. The cause of her death remained unknown."

"Could anyone have broken her and killed her other than a woman?" said Zabiba to herself, and added out loud, "Truly, a woman, if she decides to do so, will get a man by any means, and if she chooses to destroy a woman or wages a war with her in the process for one she loves, she will not hesitate to go as far as murder. They killed your mother, my king."

The king said with a weak smile, "I had to live among all that and felt that everyone who surrounded me felt animosity toward me. And that was not only true about the wives and concubines of my father but also about my younger brothers, though I had done everything possible to maintain good relationships with them. But my position as the only legitimate heir to the throne, and also the fact that my mother was the king's cousin, made everyone jealous of me, especially my brothers. For because of my position, only I was suited to be the next king, while everybody else was a step lower than I.

Among themselves they were equal by birth, no one was any higher or any better than another. They were all boys and not one of them could gain a special position over the others. Zabiba, I don't deny that I myself was not that thrilled to keep friendship with those among whom I happened to live."

"That is easy to understand, my lord. Could a bird of one species live in peace with birds of prey? Especially if it sees that their beaks are ready to feed on its flesh and drink its blood."

Zabiba said that and touched his face, not allowing herself more than that, though at times she wanted to kiss him, especially when she saw how his soul was overwhelmed, and what bitter and tormenting memories echoed within him. But she did not allow herself to kiss him, fearing it would break the thread of his thoughts and memories about his father.

"The day came when they all united against me, all the wives of my father, my brothers, and even many of the courtiers. I do not know why the courtiers took their side and why my sisters did not join my brothers."

"From what I can judge, my great king, the law does not permit women to inherit the throne, and in that way a man is over a woman in all areas. Since such is the rule, your sisters had no reason for which to hate you as did those who desired power, as well as the noblemen positioning themselves to advance their own interests."

"You are absolutely correct, Zabiba."

The king continued his story, "Before I had even reached adulthood, my father sent me far away from the palace, though he did not tell me why he was sending me away. He just told me that I would live with one of his cousins in a town away from the capitol. As I was moving, all the servants were sad, because they liked me, and tried their best to hide their tears in fear that my father's wives might see it and make their lives unbearable."

"You see, my king, how loyal common people can be? You must have treated them with dignity and respect, and so they commiserated with you and their hearts were with you when those who had influence and power united against you and when you were leaving the palace. Do you know why the influential people were happy for you to leave the palace?"

The king replied, "That is the question I cannot answer. Why did they plot to get rid of me and why were they so ecstatic as I was leaving the palace?"

"They plotted to get you out of the palace so that they could accomplish their own selfish schemes without the hindrance of a royal heir who could be the eyes of the king in his absence. They did this only when you were old enough and mature enough to become a threat to them. In your absence it was easy for any of the emirs and those who supported them to battle for the throne, since before all the emirs were equal and not one of them could be any more important than the other. After you were gone, a race for power started in which everyone had an equal chance to win, and everyone took his chances accordingly. Right?"

"You are right, Zabiba," said the king. "However, that mad race for power was the main reason why I could return to the palace and accept the kingship after the death of my father. Because the military and government officials, who had never approved of my exile in the first place, took my side and became a protection for me. With them also stood my blood relatives who never took part in the palace intrigues and had no interest in them. That is why the courtiers and those who had wanted my exile hurried to forget their plotting as soon as I had won my first battle for the right to inherit the crown, and took my side with those who supported me."

"So it happens in struggles of power. But fortunately, in matters of relationships between people which are based on the human notions of respect, dignity and love, everything is different, isn't it?"

"Again, you are right, Zabiba. And there is nothing one can do to change that. Nonetheless, so it happened that I am a king. But what I am curious to know is how is it that you can love me in such a way that my royal status does not affect you in any way?"

"That's easy, because my love has no selfish agenda, my king. And since I am not trying to pursue any goals or get something out of you, in time I will feel as if you were just like me. Nothing will interfere with my love for you, and you too will be able to love me in such a way, even though you are a king."

"Perhaps," said the king.

And Zabiba added, "As they say, 'A door will open for the one who is patiently standing before it' and 'Everyone who earnestly seeks with diligence will have his opportunity to come in.'"

The king continued his story, saying, "All of my sisters wept bitterly when I left. I will not conceal from you that my relationships with my sisters were most wonderful and most sincere. They cried bitterly over me, and at every opportune moment, when their mothers or the other women of the king did not know about it, they would come visit me. Through them, I would gain news from the palace. Obviously, I found out that after my departure the palace turned into chaos. My father was advancing in years. The conspiracies had no end, and people who were not a part of them could not tolerate that situation any longer. Evil was multiplying and the intrigues between my father's wives were continuous. Each plotted something against another in an effort to gain advantage."

"It happens among the common people as well. When all are equal and they are trying to make a decision which touches everybody's interests, everyone tries to obtain what is best for himself," said Zabiba to herself, without interrupting the king.

The king continued, "Each of the wives had a whole army behind them, consisting of concubines, courtiers and military men, even servants and cooks, and each of these followers were guarding their own interests."

"Even the cooks, my king?"

"Yes, even the cooks, Zabiba. The cooks are very important people in the palace, at least where intrigues are concerned, and especially those intrigues which end in the death of their intended target. Sometimes one of the queens would select one of the cooks and order him to make the king's favorite dish. Then she would take it to the king and tell him that she made it with her own hands because she knew how much the king loved it. And she could do that only on the day appointed for her visitation. Another cook might ruin the dish by adding extra salt in it or putting a dead rat in the meat. In that way, the efforts of one wife were thwarted by another."

"Do you mean to tell me that dead rodents take part in palace intrigues?"

"Yes, Zabiba, it happens. They even used to use live snakes, putting them in the fruit baskets. At times the king would execute the wife handing him the basket, even when the snake was not poisonous, suspecting her of intent to do him harm. It came to the point that my father the king, may Allah be merciful to him, never ate or drank anything they brought to him. Rarely did he see his wives, and even then for no longer than an hour, so that he would not have to eat or drink anything in their chambers. And in order to protect himself from intrigues the king appointed for himself one of his daughters to bring him food and drink and to watch while it was being prepared. (This particular daughter was from a concubine who had nobody left after her, and who herself had died giving birth). Thereafter the king's life became much easier, until the day came when that daughter fell in love with one of the courtiers who associated with one of the antagonistic factions. And he, taking advantage of her feelings for him, found a moment to put poison in the dish which was served to the king. As a result, my father died. Still, I did not dare to publicly accuse my sister of treason and decided to investigate the matter myself. When the truth was discovered, I found that my sister was totally innocent. But what happened to her became a good lesson for everyone, including her."

"So what was the lesson for that woman, my king?"

"That even when a woman has noble character, there may be villain who would use her for evil."

"But isn't what you could have learned from this whole story you have shared with me more important, my king?"

"Of course, Zabiba, but what exactly do you mean?"

"Don't you think that the multitude of wives and concubines that the king had was the main reason for the problems in the palace?"

"Yes, Zabiba, I do."

"Then why is it, my great king, that you do not limit yourself in acquiring them?"

"I do limit myself. You can see that, compared to the number of women that my father had, I have relatively few."

"They may be few in comparison to the way things used to be, but they are still too many according to the peoples' measure, my great king."

"You could be right, Zabiba, but kings measure things differently."

"But, my king, when the notions and norms of the king and his people become similar, a certain single-mindedness is formed. When the people and the king are of one mind, the kingdom will grow stronger and the king will become greater and all the more powerful."

"So you think that I don't need many sons to be my support in difficulties and grief when they come?"

"But could all those sons which you dream of and which you could possibly beget ever compare to the whole of the people, or even with half or a quarter of the people?"

"No, Zabiba, but that does not make sense. Why are you asking me this?"

"Because I was going to explain to you that in order to have a real defense, you need to move in a different direction. You need to motivate the people to be on your side."

"And who are the people?"

"Who are *your* people, my great king? Well, first of all, they are the soldiers of your army, but I don't mean the mercenaries and foreigners who now compose the majority of your army."

"But I can't have an army without mercenaries, Zabiba."

"It would be possible, my king, if you yourself would wish for that."

***

50

*The wise old woman told us that soon the king even began to feel jealousy toward Zabiba's husband. That is why he constantly badgered her about her marriage, though with caution.*

Zabiba would reply, "And what can I do? Think and judge for yourself. He is my husband by your own law and I am compelled to do everything he tells me to do. But what I must do as my duty does not completely reflect my own wishes."

*And when he told her that he knew that or could at least guess about it, they both laughed, considering that problem beneath their attention and as something which could not become an obstacle in their relationship. Yet, their love was not weakened.*

***

One time when Zabiba came to the king's palace, the king, who had secretly given his whole life as a prisoner due to his love of her, noticed a change in her. When he came out to meet her, his intuition, which had never betrayed him, revealed that she was not the same as she was when they last parted.

Later the king said, "Recently, I have begun to notice that something troubles you. I tried to think of everything that has happened in our relationship, but cannot find a reason for this change in you."

"I have no worries as long as I have your trust, my king."

"But I can see, Zabiba, that you *are* worried. Nothing brings joy or pleasure to your soul anymore. Nothing makes you happy. Even our relationship has become routine and habitual. And since the monotonous, day to day, perusing of the same pages of our relationship tires you, boredom has probably settled in you and burdens your heart."

"Yes, my great king, monotonous repetition does give birth to boredom, but no repetition will bring boredom if a person longs for it with all of her heart and if she reaches for it with all of her soul."

"What do you mean, Zabiba?"

"Isn't it habitual that the sun comes up every morning? Aren't we used to such things as the appearance of the moon and the blowing of the northern winds, refreshing a man? Can food and drink become boring?"

"You are right, Zabiba. All those things cannot become boring because without them there would be no life. And there is no substitute for them either. That which a man cannot live without cannot bore him or make his relationships routine."

"What do you mean by "his relationships," my king? I can see you are changing the subject from notions about general things to notions about humanity!"

"Yes, Zabiba, I am doing it so that I can try and find out what bothers you and understand how I might overcome your worries and your sad mood."

"Why are you so concerned, my king?"

"Zabiba, I don't want anything else but for you to be happy and for joy to come back into your life."

"When did you notice a change in me?"

"A few weeks ago."

"Is it because all this time our opinions would always differ at first until we could reach a common conclusion?"

"I asked myself the same question, Zabiba, but I can say, at least about myself, that the differences between us did not worry or sadden me, for to have differences of opinion is natural. Besides, our differences fade away as we get to know each other better and we form similar views about the world."

"But you cannot judge the strength, patience, and feelings of other people simply from your own perspective. For other people may not have these qualities in the same way and to the same degree that you do. So it seems that your comparison of the two of us is not valid."

"I agree, Zabiba. That is why I said to myself that no one knows Zabiba better than she herself."

"But you know me too, my king."

"I know you, but you deny my conclusions and therefore doubt that my intuition is enough to understand you correctly. But before I relent and say that my interest in your feelings has diminished because I could not find out the truth about them, I beg you to answer one question. Have I, or anyone else, caused this change in your demeanor, and if so, how and why? If you give me a straight answer, I will have an opportunity to seek a practical solution, but if not, I will have nothing but doubts and guesses tormenting me, while a resolution would be impossible. In any case, your not telling me of the reasons for your distress will mean that you reject all of my attempts to help you."

"But I already said that you have no reason to suspect that anything is wrong because I see nothing which should make you doubt. I am happy, but I am worried for our love."

"Is it my love for you that bothers you or are you doubting your own feelings?"

"No, I am confident in my feelings and I do not doubt you either. I tremble in awe when I picture the happiness which came about because of our unimaginable love. But it worries me that our love ceased being ordinary. It achieved an incredible height and left behind the boundaries of all that it is possible to see or touch, the boundaries of what can be heard or read about; it reached a height that no one else had ever achieved before."

"That which allowed us to reach that height will also help us to overcome it and reach yet other mountains. If we do not treasure that which helped us to reach this far, we won't be able to conquer new heights."

"You started using military language when you said that we will conquer heights!"

"Yes, Zabiba, because the progress of love means victory over all things that create obstacles, otherwise it will never reach new heights. It is similar to a decisive victory over an enemy who threatened what is dear to us. Isn't the lack of love in a man what weakens his position and qualities which make up the man himself? Isn't it natural for a human being to love another human being? To enjoy his role? To love people and to serve them? And are there not factors and obstacles in him and in what surrounds him which do not allow him to act naturally? They prevent him from mobilizing his energy, feelings, and talents as they interfere in his attempts to reach new heights."

"Your words are true, my king," said Zabiba, thus letting him know that he would not find out much about what was troubling her.

The king grew silent. He knew that Zabiba had not told him everything she felt and her inadequate reply to his inquiry displeased him.

He stopped in order to prevent their conversation from escalating into an argument and tried to calm himself, controlling his anger. He had been about to protest that he knew his suspicion was right, and that what she told him wasn't the true reason for her mood (even though her doubts about his love sounded like a good excuse).

He started to reason with himself, "At least I have some idea about what worries her, though she does not want to tell me everything. And in time I will be able make her happy and joyful once again. And this will bring me joy and comfort, but for now I will have to accept what I do know about this woman in hopes of eventually finding out what is on her mind. Doesn't a woman always hide her secrets from the man closest to her, while discussing them with those who are not even close? Don't women differ from men, who entrust their secrets only to those who will keep them? Women, on the other hand, tell their secrets to whomever they want, led by some inner voice in their souls. While a man will entrust his secrets to a woman, a woman rarely entrusts hers to a man, even if he is the one closest to her. A woman would rather reveal others' secrets than her own. That is why if one wants to know a woman's secret, one should go to those women that are closest to her. If a woman does not want to tell her secrets to a man who is close to her, it means that what she conceals may cause his displeasure. I can only imagine why she does not want me to find out the reasons for her worries, and has rejected my help which could have relieved her of them."

But there was nothing to add to explain Zabiba's worries (and the fact that she was a little sad, but not desperate), except for the fact that her husband, whom she had avoided for a long time by inventing different excuses, had finally forced her to intimacy.

Zabiba knew very well that her husband had legal rights to be with her, but it seemed that her relationship with the king was increasingly burdened by her relationship with her husband.

It was purely feminine curiosity which made Zabiba test the king's feelings toward her. Looking for an opportunity to verify their strength, Zabiba was thinking to herself that perhaps the best way to test the king's feelings for her was to tell him some of the aspects of her relationship with her husband, for instance, the fact that she had been forced to marry him. When she was telling him about personal things, she noticed that the king disregarded the difference in their status. At times, the king would even share his secrets with her. Each of them, it seemed, had found someone with whom they could share their troubles to relieve their souls and to lift up the weights burdening them, even though at times the king would tease Zabiba about her relationship with her husband.

The king said again, "I still perceive that you are still burdened by something, Zabiba."

"A heavy burden is on my soul, my king. Believe me, what happened took place without my consent," Zabiba answered him.

He could see that the woman was in a quandary, and started thinking to himself, "Does Zabiba want me to help her dissolve her relationship with her husband? Or is she simply trying to attract my attention to something that she thinks I am not taking seriously enough? What would happen if I openly declared my passion for her and released her from this burdensome tie with her husband? Is passion forbidden? She married against her will, but in obedience to her family, so her marriage is a decision of her family. But if she grew to love me, that is her own decision. Does not a person who makes his own decisions differ from a person who obeys other people's decisions? I must tell her. I must relieve her from this nightmare."

But then he thought, "But what if she does not want our relationship to grow into a marriage? Does she not now live with a husband with whom she is intimate?"

And then he thought, "But she may be telling the truth when she says that she is forced to have relations with her husband, doing her duty as is required because of her status. And that is an example of obedience absent feelings and desire."

But again he started teasing Zabiba, whom he loved with all his heart, reminding her of what she had with her husband.

Becoming angry, Zabiba said, "Believe me, my king, I did not feel like somebody had made love with me, but as if somebody had whipped me with lashes. What could I have done? What would you do in my place?"

The king snapped in reply, "How could I be in your place, Zabiba? A king cannot be in a woman's place."

Zabiba, indignant that the king was angry with her, replied, "A king can be like a woman."

"And how could that be, Zabiba?"

"He *would* be like a woman sleeping with a stranger if he does not lead his army to protect his state from invading foreign armies. Isn't that what they say about many of the kings around us? They refuse to revenge their marred honor for the glory of their people. Even a woman would behave differently. Do not many women fight invaders when their country is attacked by an enemy, while men are busy fighting in other battles?"

Zabiba's words angered the king, but he kept his promise that he would treat her as his equal, and answered, "If that is true about the kings around us, that is their business. If you say that those kings can switch places with women and sleep with their husbands instead of the other way around, let them change. But don't you dare to make the mistake of thinking that the same could be said about your king! And in general, in all that is connected to me, you should hold your tongue and choose your words more carefully. Do not leave the boundaries of propriety."

"Oh, so, there! Hold *my* tongue? Didn't I tell you that it is impossible for a king to speak with a common woman as if equal?"

Seeing that he had been cruel with her, the king stroked her hair, and then said to himself, "I wonder if her husband kisses her on her lips?"

And then answered his own question, "Her husband is in the service of one of the emirs. He does not love her, and therefore probably does not kiss her on the lips. Don't people only kiss those they love on the lips?"

When he confessed to her what he was thinking about, she answered him, "First of all, I want to tell you, my great king, that love is a confidence. It's the confidence of the one who loves in the one loved. Love does not submit to the laws of the classes, and therefore it is a feeling which kings also share. I fell in love with you not because you are a king. My love is an expression of my freedom and my human essence. I suppose that you also love me not because I am a queen. Love is a quality that one has, whether he be a king or a common man, a fisherman or a farmer, a general, a worker or a spy."

Zabiba shuddered when she accidentally said "a spy" and corrected herself, "No, not spies. Your spies do not fit that role, my king."

"You think that the secret agents in my kingdom have shortcomings which deny them humanity and do not allow them to love as do all the others you have mentioned?"

"No, my king, Allah forbid me to offend your spies. But *can* those spies love anyone?"

The king answered without thinking, "In any state, the secret agents are like their king. If the king can love, his agents can love also. And if the king has no human qualities allowing him to love, then his spies do not have them either."

"Yes, that is right, my king, but our spies are not like you."

"How are they unlike me?"

"They are not like you in their behavior and morality, my king. From ages past, these hands of the law have been free to do whatever they want. And those spies think that they must always hold the people under pressure."

"How is that?"

"Spies follow me everywhere so that I cannot take a breath the way I wish, as if I had neither freedom nor choice."

"Didn't you say that you are free in my palace, and that because of your love for me and my love for you, you have regained your soul? I remember you saying that you lost your soul when you married and obeyed the desires of your husband against your own will because it was your duty in the marriage which you could not escape."

"Yes, and I almost lost myself and all that is human. I did not expect that I would choose you. And the reason I chose you was not because of the royal throne but because I found in you the qualities I was looking for. Yes, my king. You gave me back my freedom, and I have gained back my humanity."

"So, what has happened now?"

"My freedom is threatened, my great king. Am I not free to be in bed with my husband?" asked Zabiba.

"Of course you are free, if that is what you want," answered the king.

"Yes, I want to be with my husband if you are against it. But his advances are something that is forced upon me, and I want to resist them because I want to, not because you are forcing me to resist them."

"So, tell me Zabiba, is this how a common man's soul functions? Is the will of the king that burdensome for the people?"

"Yes, my king, because if the king becomes one of us, he will give us freedom, but if he is not one of us, he will impose his will upon us. And we prefer those who are like we are."

"It happened then that I fell in love with someone who is unlike me."

"That is not true, my king. You loved the one who is like your very essence that is limited by the royal crown and hidden deep inside you. As for me, I do not have a royal crown, and I would not be able to wear one even if I wanted to."

"And do you want to have a crown, Zabiba?"

"Yes, my great king, I desire to have it and I desire to have you. But I want to have both of you separately, not indistinguishable from one another. I need the crown only if you become its master rather than its prisoner. I don't want the crown to preside over your head while you are its hostage. I want you to rise above me but also to be near me and to be in my soul. I want you to be the conscience of the people, its symbol, and its heroic knight, not a symptom of its weakness. I want the crown to be your symbol, not your master and your chains. I want us, you and I, to be two souls in one body and the crown to be the symbol of our honor, not of our shame. In that case, your crown won't possess me, but on the contrary will free me and will be on my head if I possess it as you do. You will preside over me, above the crown. And above you and me will be our freedom, the ideals of our state, our nation, and our people."

After listening to what Zabiba had to say, the king said, "I grew to love you so that I could elevate both your honor and mine with a love that is sincere in all its beauty and in its full meaning, but not so that one of us would become weak. That is why I do not wish to share you with a man whom you do not want, and that is why I do not think he has any part in our life."

Zabiba said, "You are both right and wrong, my great king, and forgive me if I speak with some arrogance. But who is your friend: the one who tells you the truth or the one who agrees with whatever you say?"

The king said, "The one who tells the truth, Zabiba. What do you mean to say by this?"

"I chose you in accordance with your laws which leave me the freedom of choice. I also chose you so that with my love, I could elevate your honor. I am opening the door for you to receive the love of your people. The people will love you only when they realize that you love them. The love of the people, not the crown, strengthens your honor, my king. If you think that you can elevate my honor by merely bringing me closer to yourself without love and freedom, and that the love of your people will come to you as soon as they find out that you accepted one of their daughters, you are sorely mistaken, my king. That way you will not love the people, and you will not love me, and I will not love you because in that case, we will become two different people, each a part of his own surroundings. It will be like in my relationship with my husband, who does not acknowledge my essence and treats me as a thing. Imagine, my king, how it would feel to be treated like a thing? Wouldn't one rebel and try to find a way to exercise her right of choice?"

"Yes, of course."

"I chose you so that I could use my freedom by my own choice and will. That way, I can express myself in our relationship. By having a relationship with a common woman, you also express yourself. However, when your spies always follow me and you get angry because I have relations with my husband, my relationship with you becomes a burden. You deprive me of my freedom and do not allow me to express my human essence the way I want to. You are becoming like my husband and now I have the right to seek..." She suddenly stopped herself.

"Seek another man? Is that it?"

"Forgive me, my king. It is because love strengthens the one who loves deeply that it gives her freedom to think and make decisions. It also strengthens in her such high qualities as honesty, virtue, courage, sincerity, and faith in the right cause."

Zabiba lifted her head which she had kept down while she was saying all that. "Not many kings draw from these qualities."

"Yes, Zabiba, not many. But throughout history, all the great kings of our state who had glory and strength drew from these very qualities. Or at least some of them."

"You say glory and strength throughout history, but not all kings gained their name in the history of our kingdom because of their glory and strength. Yet the ones that did attain glory did so because they made those qualities the basis of their reign. But, my king, isn't it the people who are most important in history? Isn't it the people who by their very essence are inseparable from these qualities, and by their glorious history, they are the ones that inspired the kings on to glory?"

The king said, "Yes, Zabiba, you said it correctly. It does not really matter whether it was the people that inspired these qualities or if the king himself found a different source, whatever it might be. If the good qualities did not appeal to the people, the kings could not have found glory in doing the good deeds. Besides, a king cannot do great deeds alone without a great people and a great nation behind him. Doesn't the peak of a great mountain rely on its base and its slopes?"

"Wonderful, my king. You are the king, but now you *often* speak like we do, and often understand things the same way that we do. That is why I fell in love with you, my great king. Yes, a great king finds glory by his great deeds, but all of his deeds are done by and through the people."

"Why do you say only "often?" asked the king, much surprised. "For I do speak and understand things the way you do, don't I?"

"Yes, my king, lately you have often spoken and understood things the way we do, and that is enough for now, because you are at least able to see things from another point of view. I say "often" and not "always" because if you really understood, acted and felt the people's way, you would leave this world and go into a different one. You would not be in our world and certainly not in the world of the kings. That other world is much like the world of the gods, except that your gods are made of material objects and nothing else. Doesn't the king who understands everything and acts and feels like the people and the sons of the nation become like one of the gods? And aren't the gods an incarnation of the people's qualities, the conscience of the nation, the feelings of the poor man? Shouldn't these qualities be evident in a strong and just king who loves his people? Then gifts will be presented to him because he makes his people happy and eases their hardships."

"Zabiba, you said that I often, even though not always, think like you and that you loved me for that. And what will happen if I will reach perfection in the qualities in which I am like the people?"

"If you develop these qualities to perfection, you will become a god or one like a god, my great king, and then I won't be able to love you, and so I would not want you to be that way."

"I understand why you would not be able to love me in that case, but wouldn't you want me to become like a god?"

"Because I am a human being, my king, and love you as a man, I want you to be a man in flesh and blood, so that I could love you as a woman loves a man and would not need to worship you."

"Couldn't one combine both the elements of the human and the divine at the same time, Zabiba?"

"No, my great king. In that case, people would be worshipping a god-man. But if people elevate and worship human qualities on the basis of faith, then you will be a king who is loved as much as a god."

"I love you, Zabiba, even in spite of your sharp tongue. And do you know why?"

"No, forgive me, my king, but I don't know why."

"I fell in love with you so that my soul would not wither and so that I would not depart from real life. I wanted to remain close to the people, so that I could be a part of it and lead it after me. I do not want to become one of the gods that stand in the holy places and who receive promises from those presenting their requests. I want to live with you, and among you and meet sunrises with you. I wish that together, we could breath the air and the aroma from the palm trees and smell roses, and pray for those who have left to go to the other world, and I want to overcome treason and all that is evil."

While the king was saying all that, Zabiba listened peacefully, but when he got to the word "treason" she shuddered. She muttered, "Don't most kings love treason? Don't they plot intrigues and treason in the corridors of their palaces and even in the chambers of their wives and concubines? No, in our kingdom, or at least in our king, there is none of the treachery that is in other kings. In his qualities he is more like us."

Then she continued, already out loud, "When a king who is more like his people in his qualities reigns, then the qualities that make him closer to his people are challenged as he forgets the hardships of his youth and as his kingly pride takes him over. Only if the king remains faithful to the cause of his people, and only if he fights with his very sword and risks his royal title for it, will he take us to the heights of glory."

The king guessed what Zabiba had in mind and said to her, "I already understand what I need to do in order to express my human essence, so I will not turn from this path. And if you find treachery anywhere in this kingdom, it won't be coming from the throne. Or maybe a better way to say it, you will not find it among the sons of our kingdom."

"But I am afraid of your shaitan, my king. For it is the shaitan who plots treason. But does it not reside in each of us, my king? Because we put both of our shaitans together, now they can take over and make you betray your cause; also, the shaitan that sits in me can make me betray you, however the shaitan of the people is not strong enough to betray the people. Or to put it differently, the souls of the people are stronger, while the souls of the kings are weaker. If a king is harboring false illusions, the shaitan whispers into his ear that he could even lose his throne unless he uses treachery to save his position. Then, the king gives in to the shaitan because of his weakness and the temptation. The same happens when relatives attempt to seize the throne."

While Zabiba was saying the last phrase, she noticed a suspicious movement behind the curtain. At that moment, the king was facing her and did not see what was happening behind his back. Suddenly, a man jumped out of the curtain, brandishing a sword.

Zabiba screamed, "Look out, my king!" and rushed forward to shield him with her own body. She recognized the man who tried to kill the king as his cousin, the general of his army. Zabiba's chest happened to be closer to the sword in the decisive moment. She slid slowly to the floor and screamed, "There it is, treason in the king's house, my great king!"

The king struck the traitor first and killed him with a single heavy blow to the head. In the corner, one of his wives was ready to accept the news about the king's death.

The king rushed back to Zabiba, embraced her, kissed her, and said, "Didn't I say that you would never betray me, Zabiba, and that the shaitan could never overcome you?"

"No, no, I won't betray you. Only those who lie and who share power with them, their emirs, betray kings."

"The shaitan prompted them to do what they did, but they failed."

"Be careful, my king. What would happen if one of the emirs or one of those in power plots against you and sends an assassin with a knife, this time one out of the people, who cannot resist the shaitan? Truly, my king, the power is Iblis[*] himself."

From that day, the king swore to live for the people and for its sake, and that he would trust

---

[*] *EDITOR'S NOTE:* Iblis - Muslim personal name for the Devil, much like Satan.

neither king nor emir, not even the keepers of the royal scepter and the royal seal. He swore to live away from the palace and never to enter his forsaken house, and to burn incense in the fields and on the tombs of the sons of the people.

*****

The king was not harmed as a result of the treacherous plot, but Zabiba had received a serious wound in her chest from the blade of the sword. Now, she was lying in the chamber of the king. The doctors took care of her and the king would not leave her until the treatment was finished. He even slept in the room next to her so that she could always be near him, while he could visit her frequently to inquire about her health. When Zabiba was feeling stronger, she would speak with the king, or he himself would start a conversation. After a few days, while she was lying in bed, Zabiba said, "What are you planning to do about this?"

"About what?" asked the king.

"About the conspiracy to kill you and overthrow the throne, of course."

"I have not decided yet."

"Well, our enemies have already decided what to do and have obviously set their plan in motion. You need to think of how you are going to resist them because, you can rest assured, they will repeat their attempts. They attacked first, trying to stop you before you could fulfill your intentions."

"But the one who tried to kill me is already dead."

"The one you killed was only a claw in one of the enemy's paws, my king, but all those who desire to kill you and to take over your kingdom are still alive, including those who are ready to help the traitors do it."

"You are right, Zabiba, but what can we do?"

"You need to appoint someone to investigate this conspiracy to find out how deep it goes and how large it is. Only after you find that out will you be able to clearly assess the situation. Right now, it is hard to determine anything about it. Maybe even this messenger or that doctor are a part of this conspiracy," she said, indicating them with her finger.

"Why would they join the conspiracy, Zabiba?"

"Truly, the one whose soul is empty could be pursuing his base goals, confident in the worthiness of his cause. Then whatever goal he might have would be a good enough reason to be a part of this conspiracy."

"Even a messenger, Zabiba? What kind of interest could a royal messenger have if he were to join the traitors?"

"My king, I brought them up just as an example, to alert your attention. I do not accuse anybody yet; I was just imagining possibilities. You can imagine some circumstances yourself and then judge whether or not it is possible. But of course mere suspicion is not as good as knowing for certain. I only took the people whom you appointed to look over me as an example.

"As for the verdict, my king, that is what the prosecutors and the judge should announce when they find enough evidence to declare the suspects guilty. As for the messenger and his interests in joining a conspiracy, I can tell you that he is a good example to scrutinize. The one who is tempted by a higher position and cannot rise to it may try to reach it through a fall."

"Do you want to conduct an investigation and a hearing, Zabiba?"

"Absolutely, my king. Isn't that the best way to expose a conspiracy and catch the traitors?"

"Yes, but if we do it so openly, the news about our assault will spread far beyond the walls of the palace. Then others will find out that somebody already attempted to conspire against the king and will start new conspiracies."

"Indeed, they will know everything to the last detail in living colors, as it truthfully was. That is better than hiding it. Bad things don't disappear just because nobody notices them. Any situation of this sort needs to be addressed. It is better if the people hear the bad news from the interested party, especially if the news relates to power. If we leave people in darkness and ignorance, anybody who wishes could spread the seeds of untrue rumors among the people that will penetrate their ears and sprout in their minds."

"But isn't it better to bury the corpse instead of letting it stay on the ground, Zabiba?"

"Of course, my great king. But sometimes when people kill an animal, they leave its corpse for a while for people to see and only then bury it. They do it so that nobody spreads the rumor upon seeing a new grave, that another slave was murdered and then buried secretly."

"Yes, but to solve this riddle is not easy."

"Yes, my king, not at all easy, but it is your riddle and you must solve it. You need to know when, how, and by whom these things were conspired."

"That's right, Zabiba, but the path is hard and at times thorny."

Zabiba answered, "That is the very role and responsibility of the king and his regime. His path is hard and thorny when he does not accept any single side, quality, or color, for colors and shades change constantly along with the colors of life, its themes, and directions of movement. But the king's path is yet harder and thornier if he does not want to blend in and change along the other colors, if his movements and rhythm do not correspond to the movements and rhythm of life around him, if he chooses just one color and distinguishes it from all others; if that color becomes the main distinction of his personality, and if he chooses for himself the movements and the rhythm which will be convenient for him alone."

Then the king said, "Let it be! I will order someone to get to the bottom of this."

"If you allow me, my king, I would ask you to arrest all who knew about the preparation of the assassination and did not warn you about it as well as all those who may have taken part in the plot."

"I killed one of them, the man who wanted to kill me and wounded you when you, my love, received the blow which was intended for me, my devoted and faithful Zabiba."

"One. That was just one poisoned dart, my great king. That is why you need to find the bow and the quiver full of arrows that were not used because the traitors did not yet have an opportunity or need to put them to work."

"But Zabiba, the murderer had a sword in his hand, not a bow."

"I am speaking only figuratively, my king. All the elements of my allegory mean people involved in this conspiracy. One arrow is a person, many arrows, many people. The quiver could mean those who organized and prepared this vicious attack. The bow stands for their plot and the methods they chose to reach their goals."

"Oh, now I understand, Zabiba! We will definitely get to the truth after we appoint people to do the investigation and throw all the suspects into prison."

Then Zabiba added, "In that case, we will have to arrest some of those who are close to us, because if we don't do that, they will attack us again in desperation. One of them is an accomplice to the murderer. There can be no doubt about that."

"But I did not see anybody with that man."

"Your wife, the queen, was with him, far from her quarters. She came with him secretly. She had some role in what was about to happen."

"But could a woman be part of the plot like this?"

"Yes, my great king. The parts in a plot are shared by all participants. If there is a role for a man, there is a role for a woman."

The king said, "I had noticed her, but I thought she was there by chance. Or rather, I did not ask myself at that moment why she would happen to be there."

Zabiba said, "Some kings doubt everything and everyone. Because they have no convictions left, there is no basis for their thoughts. They are tortured by doubts as if they were seeing life and its ways for the first time. We do not want you to be like that. But there are some who do not listen to their souls and do not observe their surroundings."

"Do I fit that description, Zabiba?"

"No, my king, god forbid me to think so! I would punish myself if I were to offend you unjustly. But what made you ignore the possible treacherous role of the queen was caused by your very doubt that she could have any role in such a plot. And that is because you could not, under any circumstances and in any situation, imagine that she might be your enemy. Also, your confidence in the absolute nature of your power kept you from taking protective measures. Because of your complacency, you were lured into a trap. You also think that if you accept or reject something in your relationships with other people, those people will do the

same. Without enough experience, it is easy to mis-
judge people, for not all people are like the one who
reigns over them. They will be bad if they are
treated badly, and obedient if you treat them well,
but your influence on their qualities will be very
limited.

"You ignored the queen as a person and left
her for the sake of the other wives and concubines.
That is why you did not pay attention to her presence and did not take pains to ask her why she
happened to be there. You did not grant her any
real attention and acted as if she were a mere thing.
Or to put it better, you looked at her as if she were
one of those who are supposed to be behind a curtain in order to appear before you, to serve your
wishes, to take care of the guests, or to guard you.
You did not look at her as one looks at the queen or
even as one of your wives."

"So, Zabiba, you think that I need to arrest
her and throw her in prison?"

"No, my great king, if you don't mind, I would
suggest that you don't put her into prison, but in
some secluded place. Her case stinks like a corpse
that needs to be buried immediately. I think that
the best thing would be keeping her in the palace,
but not in your private chambers. Let somebody
serve her, but it cannot be anybody from her own
maids. The one serving her should have strict instructions from my lord. Most importantly, these
instructions must be formulated in terms of what is
permitted rather than what is forbidden. If the one
responsible for her has any questions, he must
immediately come to the king."

"And why can't it be given in terms of what is
forbidden?"

"Because if you state what is forbidden, then
the boundaries of what is permitted are broadened
to infinity and everyone can interpret the bounda-

ries however they wish to. Besides, if you tell what is forbidden, everybody who is interested would consider it his duty to add new forbidding rules. You can forbid things, of course, but not in this particular case, my king. Prohibiting things is possible if you are thinking of a law for the people. Then, the people have a broader field for action and thoughts, and they know what is forbidden to them, and having learned what not to do, they would not break the law."

"But why can't I leave her own servants to wait on her? Why do I have to find new ones?"

"Because up until this moment she was treated as a queen," said Zabiba. "As a queen she had a great influence over people, especially on those who served her. Even when she is placed in her new location which you choose for her, people who used to treat her like a queen and who formed certain relationships with her will act towards her according to her title and will obey her orders either willingly or unwillingly. If she commands them, they will let her go out anywhere she wants and they will let everybody she wants to see come visit her. She might even be able to spy on you. Don't queens spy on kings?"

The king laughed, and Zabiba answered him with a smile.

"You are incredibly clever, Zabiba!"

Zabiba replied, "Life taught me that, my king."

The king said, "I live this life too, and I am older than you are, but I do not know the things you know, even though everything you say is right in front of my eyes. But it is only when you explain things that I understand that all you say is true."

"Forgive me, my great king, for being so direct with you. If you think that I have crossed the borders of propriety, do pardon me. I appeal to the meekness of your character and to your kindness."

After saying this, Zabiba added to herself, "Don't people ask for kings' forgiveness, praising and worshipping them full of submission and obedience, independently of whether or not they deserve mercy?"

"Speak Zabiba."

"I have seen life with all of its beautiful and bitter moments. When I choose something in life because it pleases me in some way, I can rarely have what I want, or if I happen to get something, it turns out to be only a small portion of what I really desire. And even that small portion comes after many sacrifices, unsuccessful attempts and a tormenting wait. I spend so much time outside that my skin is burned by summer heat and winter frost. Every day of my life I have to deal with people with whom I did not want to have anything in common and walk down paths which I would never have taken of my own volition. The worst of all is that I have no freedom of choice. Your life looks very different. You rarely see any daylight; direct sun rays hardly ever touch you, and if you happen to feel a little chill, someone immediately brings you covers or one of your women comes to warm you with her body and to make a drink which makes one's body hot and because of which one's soul flies away."

"I came to live in this palace only recently but before that I lived away from all this."

"Yes, my lord, but you lived in yet another palace where you were treated as an emir, and now you are treated as a king. You never had and never will have the pleasure of living among people. You have never become acquainted with the ways of the common people. The way they speak, for instance. At times they honestly and openly, hiding no secret interests, tell you "no." Your servants are always agreeing with you because they are trying to get something out of you. Isn't it true that most of those who live in the palace flatter the king when he is at the peak of his power and try to destroy him as soon as he is weak?"

"Yes, there is some truth to that. One might say that that was exactly the case with my exile, coronation, and this conspiracy against me. But is it honorable to be a common citizen? Isn't to be a king more honorable than to be a subject, Zabiba?"

"The pride in being a citizen and the responsibility to one's state are much more honorable, because they define honor, my king. It can neither be inherited nor received as a prize. No honor is real if it is not gained by one's faithfulness to his country and his understanding that his main honor is in the values of the country to which he belongs, its nation and its people, and in doing one's responsibilities and duty. The one who possesses this quality will carry his banner with honor. To be a king is an honor too, but the people do not consider anything honorable which does not correspond to the notions which we just discussed, I mean the patriotism of a citizen to his country and in his duty.

"I lived a kind of life, my king, which you did not have. You have never experienced life as it flows away from the burdens and sins of the palace. So now when you achieve anything in this life, you act like a beginner who is recording on his scorecard a victory which a pro let him have, sharing from his vast account, or as a child who is taught by his father how to play a game. You enjoy your successes, and it is true that your actions at times do lead to victories. These victories have little value, however, because they do not result from your own work and abilities, gained by the method of trial and error, take-offs and falls, in other words, by hard lessons."

"What do you know about me, Zabiba?"

"In spite of the form of which you are an expression, your essence could turn you in such a direction that you found it possible and even natural to speak with me, a devoted representative of the people, my great king!"

"That's true, but you speak about me as if I were isolated from my subjects and as if I never saw them."

"The main thing is not for you to see them, my lord. The main thing is for them to live in your conscience and for you to know them. You need to live among them to understand when and why they agree and when and why they disagree with you. You need a kind of experience which would make you one of them while you rule them."

"But I used to have to meet common people very often when I lived away from this palace, with guards, gardeners, and at times with cooks."

"Suppose, my king, you had to meet with them."

"But that is true, I really did have to meet with them."

"Forgive me, my lord. I don't accuse you of lying to me; I do not doubt the truthfulness of your words. Even though most kings are liars and deserve to be taken with much suspicion, I believe that right now you are speaking the truth. I used the word 'suppose' when I said 'suppose you had to meet with them' because I was trying to tell you that there is a difference between a situation when an emir meets a commoner from time to time and a situation where a person actually lives among the people. You would meet with a guard who greeted you and made you feel like an emir. You would meet, or rather, pass by a field worker who would freeze in a bow before you, acknowledging your position as an emir. You would meet with a cook, but only because you needed to make orders about your meal. Have you ever struck anybody or ever taken a blow because somebody was teaching you how to fight, so that after being knocked off your feet you would rise up and hit the offender to knock him out in his turn? Have you ever tried to walk barefoot on the ground to find out how it feels and what the poor have to suffer? Have you ever been hungry and unable to find any food? Have you ever known famine? Have you ever had to borrow money to buy a piece of bread for your family, or paid a rent for your house, so that you would know the afflictions of the needy? And have you ever tried to convince a woman, like a common man, that you are worthy to sleep with her, that your relationship would grow stronger if you did so? In your case, does the woman who is supposed to sleep with you even have the right to decline?"

"As for the last question, she does have a choice to agree or decline."

"But do all women in the king's palace have the same conditions of life, so that any woman could deny a king's wish? What happens if a woman does not wish to sleep with you?"

The king answered, "The main thing is that she is free to decline."

"No, not so, my great king, the one you want will eventually be yours. It never happens that thousands of kings would compete to have her, as our men compete over us. The king is always one. And when competition is replaced with monopoly, there is no freedom of choice. If you eliminate freedom by presenting no other alternatives, you must be selling some bad goods."

"Am I bad goods, Zabiba?"

"No, my king, but you have a legal right to make people's lives better. You can become an influential and mighty leader. And I want to be your faithful helper, who will support you in all your endeavors. And if we both fail, I will simply go back to my normal life and my former state, and you will join the army of kings whom I called 'bad goods.'

"You have decided to leave me, haven't you, Zabiba?"

"No, my lord, not at all. I decided to always support you, from the moment you let me be beside you, and I have already had an opportunity to show my faithfulness to you. I am a part of my people, and I carry their conscience by my commitment to them. If we fail, that means that you have left me. And that will happen if you choose one road while your people choose another, and you stay with the kings while I return to the people."

"But common people are not always right, Zabiba."

"Yes, but aristocrats are not always right either, my king, even according to your measurements. Only the common opinion of the people as a whole, as the quintessence of its being, turns out to be true. That is only possible when the people have the right to utilize their freedom, while the aristocrats carry the full responsibility for their deeds, my lord. As to some special cases and exceptions to this rule, that's a topic for another time. And you can imagine what the united opinion of the people would be of a king who takes no interest in their affairs. In that opinion they would be right."

"What would make people trust their king?"

"The key to their trust is honesty. The king must be honest to himself and to his people as he fights for the people's interests, and not his own interests. He must create a tie between his own conscience and that of the people as he rejoices and grieves with them. He must give all of himself to the people, forsake his own wishes, and learn from the people to be their equal."

"But that is not just one quality, but a whole multitude of them," said the king.

"Yes, my king. Though your faith must be the most profound quality of them all, there are a multitude of them. Is one quality alone enough to be a king?"

"Isn't a king the top of the pyramid and the head of his people?"

"Will the top of the mountain be the top if it has no distinction from the slopes? If one supposes that one quality is enough to be a king, how can he require of people so many positive qualities which would make them worthy to be his subjects?"

"And what are the positive qualities which I should require from my subject?"

"He must obey you and not betray you. He must follow your orders and join your army if you command him to do so. He must fight and never retreat, that is, he must be brave. He must not protest when you take away his land to give it to your emirs or to keep for your own possession. All these qualities, my great king, are required of your subjects, yet you, who are at the top of power want just one good quality to make you into a good king."

"Your tongue is much too sharp!"

"I know that and that is why I ask for your forgiveness. I appeal to your kindness, not in fear of your whip, but in order for you to understand what role I carry. I want you to become so great that I could be proud of being with you, and your people would be proud that you are their king. And now tell me, my king, what would you do if one of the sons of the people were worthy to carry a title of a king or emir? Is it not established that only a king's son or brother could become a king's heir? That's why at times the situation becomes both ridiculous and terrible. Why do we think that a king's son is any better than a son of a common man? Why is it that a king's son gets his throne just for the virtue of being his son? Why do his uncles and brothers get power by birth rights, and not according to their abilities, and not by fair competition in their service to the people and the state? They have to earn the right to rule in the eyes of the whole people."

"But truly a son of a commoner cannot possibly rule, Zabiba!"

"Why is that, my king?"

"How can a carpenter, a blacksmith, a farmer, a tradesman or a soldier manage the matters of the state?"

"They all could do it very well, my great king, and perhaps better than some of the kings and emirs, for they are prone to be very responsible. They could do it if you create for them the same conditions and opportunities that a king's heir or an emir has. I dare say that from my point of view virtually all of these people would do better than any emir. But because in their position they lack in equipment, if competing in the same race with the emirs they could never win. In the end of that race it would look as if the son of a commoner did not weather the trial while the emir and the heir overcame him in a great victory. Those in power interpret this as an inherent inability of common people to govern. It would be the same if large and wealthy tradesmen were to compete with the people new to business. Which group, do you think, would win that contest and possess all the markets and goods? Even if we try this contest in the area of trade business with theoretical equality, some of the participants would be able to completely eliminate others from the start by means of monopolizing and competition. Would that kind of contest be a fair way of judging the abilities of either? Imagine, my king, what the results would be if some of the tradesmen who now have the influence and support from the government could not use it for the competition. A wealthy tradesman is guaranteed to have victory over a small merchant because of the power he receives through bribing influential politicians."

The king answered, "It is certainly true that if conditions are not equal everything happens as you described it and that everybody achieves very different results."

"Yes you can compare this example with any other situation where a fight of power is at stake while the resources are divided unevenly. That would give you an answer to your question as to whether or not a commoner could manage the affairs of the state."

"So, what should we do then, Zabiba?" asked the king.

"You need to become a living particle of the people, its conscience, thoughts and deeds. Through dialogue and meditation you will gain understanding of what is right in your deeds and thoughts. You need to learn about life in all its gory details, as it is in reality, and not how it has been presented to you so far, much embellished by those who are the mediators between you and life. Forsake the institute of inheritance by blood and allow the inheritance to be claimed by all who are sincere and capable. Establish a law that nobody can become an emir because he happens to be born in a certain time and place, but instead that only those who are worthy can wear the title justly. Make it so that twenty or thirty men have that title and privileges, and so that those who aspire to it are chosen out of the most capable and respected individuals, including some from the common people, and so that all may compete for the title on an equal basis. Compensate these emirs with a monthly allotment from the government, to prevent them from attempting to rob the people and in order to protect the nation from their greed."

"But why not let them trade and do other things that they were doing before when they were among the people, so that they could support themselves rather than waiting for the state to do it?"

"Because they would start robbing the people, my great king, instead of working for the people. They would exploit rather than taking care of them. Only those who have equal opportunities, who know that they have a fair chance of success, can work freely and honestly. Can a common man compete with an emir? They will start from different points and will reach different results which will not be caused by what they deserved or by success in a just competition."

"I agree with you," said the king, and added, "And what if the king dies or is killed in war? Who then will assume the crown?"

"In that situation it will be necessary to gather all the emirs so that they choose the best among themselves, according to the established plan for that circumstance. If everybody is equal and free in their choice, they will be able to choose the best among them."

"And what would we do with the problem of the lack of experience among them?" asked the king.

"You need to prepare them in equal measure, as you would do if you were going to form a counsel to help you in making decisions in the questions of power. You need to participate in all the decisions which this counsel makes."

"In other words, you are suggesting that I change the power structure of the kingdom and destroy the kingdom to the last stone of its foundation. Even if I accept your suggestion, how could somebody with the title of an emir carry out the responsibilities belonging to the king? Emirs are not equal with kings to sit beside them and make independent decisions."

"I do not want to destroy the foundation of your kingdom; I suggest building a new foundation. For if the foundation is not firm, how can one build a sturdy structure on it? If we want to build a sturdy structure which would protect us with a reliable shield, we need to rebuild the foundation. Because the council of emirs and nobility will not issue their decisions from your name, but from their own. Some of your decisions will be issued under the name of the council and others independently, even when you use other people's advice in making them, so that all decisions are based on dialogue and are balanced and careful. I have heard people say that in some kingdoms emirs preside with the kings as equals. And most of the decisions are made from their name, as if they were equal, but in reality everything is quite different. Some emirs and kings manage to make decisions directed against the people and the nation and that brings shame on them and on their nations. Sometimes they let foreign armies rule their nations and give some of their property to foreigners. They themselves make those decisions, and then tell the people that the decision was made by a council of emirs, on whom the fate of the people and the kingdom supposedly depends.

"Isn't that strange, my king? My god, if the kings were to be just a little transparent and show their people just a small portion of the flexibility that they demonstrate when dealing with the foreign kings (which is nothing else but fawning) their crowns would remain their own, and the people would praise them while they lived and bear their coffins on their hands after they die."

"And will my people praise me if I do and honor me after my death?"

"Yes, my king, after you have lived a long and prosperous life, the people will carry you on their hands. You will live in their hearts and they will keep and protect you."

After saying this, Zabiba thought to herself, "How often do kings arrange for their death while they are still in power! Instead of doing good and earning a place near our Lord in the heavens, they try to get something for themselves now, while they are still alive. They are godless both in their life and after death. So why would God be merciful to them?"

Zabiba said the last phrase out loud, and the king heard it.

"Zabiba, do you believe in a god who is not among our gods?"

"Yes, my lord. I believe in the only God, the god who created you and whom you did not create. I do not believe in gods whose images are crafted by a carpenter, a smith, or a mason."

"And what does the god you worship look like, Zabiba? Is he bigger than the gods we make out of stone and marble, and forge out of gold and silver, depending on what each of us can afford?"

"No, my king. My God is immaterial."

"Does he have white skin like the kings which come to us from the far away lands, or dark skinned like our slaves? Or is he tanned like most of our people? Or some other color?"

"He is Allah, my great king, and he, may his name be praised, is the light which fills the sky and all the lands. It is he by whose will everything on the earth was created."

"Maybe he is a blacksmith or a carpenter? Or...? I mean, how did he make everything? What is his trade?"

"His trade is power and majesty, which contain everything in themselves, my king."

"But how can one being create all these things around us, Zabiba?"

***

A servant knocked on the door, asking for permission to come in. He brought a brew made from flowers in a pot and some sweetener. He and the person accompanying him came in and froze in the presence of the king, for according to the custom of that time they could depart only after they had performed all their duties in serving the king.

Zabiba turned around and with a wink said to him, "The servants are not going away; probably they are waiting for your permission to leave."

When the king noticed that Zabiba winked at him, he felt embarrassment, for no one had ever winked at him before. Among the people, winking either meant flirting or trying to call attention to something which has not been noticed by the another. In the king's circles, nobody winked because the kings have no need to wink in order to flirt or warn someone; they have other means for doing that. Also, kings are free to communicate properly without any signs because nobody puts a lock on their mouth or forbids them to express their wishes. They can openly express their admiration toward those around them and have no need to wink as Zabiba just did.

The king told his servants to go.

Then the second servant said that they came to serve the king and to find out if there is anything else the king desires and whether or not he liked the brew when he tried it.

Zabiba winked at the king again and said, "If the king has already told you to leave, just set the brew on the table, and if the king needs anything else done for him, I can serve him. I have recovered from my injury sufficiently and can serve the king very well myself."

The king nodded to his servants and told them to leave.

When they left, and one of them was probably still near the door, the king wanted to take a sip from the goblet, but Zabiba was faster than his hand and whispered into his ear, "No, my lord! I beg you, do not drink this."

The king was taken by surprise by her fast move and asked, "Why shouldn't I drink it?"

"I will explain everything to you."

When the sound of footsteps made by the servants became distant she whispered in his ear, "I fear that this may be a new poisonous arrow, which is intended to kill you and me as well."

"But a chamomile brew is not an arrow!"

"I am speaking figuratively, only using the arrow as a comparison meaning that it is a new attempt, this time to poison you and me, and that way end your life and that of the one who could become a witness and reveal somebody's evil intents to people. But to replace our doubts with certainty, send this brew to someone you trust and find out whether there is something harmful in it."

The king said, "Alright, Zabiba, so shall we do."

After a while the results from this examination came and it turned out that the brew was indeed poisoned. After hearing what was reported, he turned to Zabiba and said, "If it was not for you, Zabiba, your king would be dead now. If it was not for you, my love, I swear by god, I'd be gone forever."

"I beg you, say instead, 'If it were not for the mercy of Allah who made us fall in love with each other, we all would be gone for a long time now.' Isn't the people the shield and the sword of the kingdom? And the king, isn't he the symbol of its blossom, its wisdom, conscience and glory among other nations? Isn't the king the hand that carries the banner of his people and their pride at all times? Didn't I tell you, my great king, that Allah protects the righteous and that the people are the protectors of the king's house, his pure and right word and deed, and his ability to create?"

"Yes, I swear by Allah that if it were not for Allah and the people, we would all be gone," said the king.

Zabiba was glad when she noticed that the king swore by Allah for the very first time. She had never heard him do that before.

***

Zabiba finally recovered from the wound completely. Now she went back and forth between her home and the palace, rode her white horse* and wore beautiful clothes that the king gave her, or which she bought at the marketplace. Every time when she was leaving the palace, she greeted the guards at the gates, but didn't just nod her head or lift her hand as do the emirs, noblemen, and courtiers, but answered their greetings with words. She would stop by the gate to find out how one soldier or another was doing if she had not seen him at the post for a long time. And if they told her that he was sick, she would visit him at home or send him a bouquet of roses, which she would pick in the palace garden. When she was leaving the pal-

---

* *EDITOR'S NOTE:* "The old gray mare, She ain't what she used to be!"

ace, the one accompanying her would be bringing out treats and sweets from the king's table. And when she was coming to the palace, she carried things that she had bought for them. She would question the workers in the king's garden about their life and if she saw among them an old man bent by the many years of his life and the hardships of poverty, she would tell him to take a rest and not to work for a few days. She treated the servants the same way. Everyone in the palace except for the emirs, princesses, nobility, and former counselors of the king were glad about what Zabiba did and spoke of her with much love. Good rumors about her spread far beyond the palace walls.

When Zabiba came home, her husband would meet her with more joy than usual. Also now, because of her notoriety and influence, he desired her even more than before. But each day, she felt more and more that she was torn into pieces, especially when she was in bed with her husband.

"Doesn't the soul live apart from the body?" she would ask herself, and then answer, "Most beautiful is a person whose soul dwells with her body. Isn't a person from his very birth a soul living in the flesh? Isn't the soul separated from the body only after death? Is the look of a dead man more attractive than the look of one alive? Now, I am dead in my house, and my corpse is decaying when I am in bed with my husband, for my soul is away from me at that time. My soul, bodiless and imperfect, is there with the king. And even though it is glowing so that the king's soul would become clear and whole, still it seems that my soul is lacking something which could make it complete. And since I'm starting to feel this division acutely, I realize that the time has come for radical action. I need to make a decision which will reunite my soul and my body and which will allow me to acquire my best form. Don't people in heaven live in the form of souls, pleasing Allah, praising him, and are they not in their best condition by his will?"

***

The next time Zabiba came back to the palace and sat by the king, the king told her, "Last time the servants who came in with the flower brew interrupted our conversation."

"What were we talking about, my king?"

"We were talking about your god, Zabiba."

"Oh, yes, we were talking about that. You see, my king, how life distracts people even from God?"

The king said, "Yes, I have not seen my god for a whole week already. And all because it is in the hall closet, the key to which has gotten lost in the palace some place, or for some other reason. I don't know for sure."

"I, on the other hand, can see my God every second, and not in any set day or hour, my great king."

"How can you see him, Zabiba? You are in the palace behind its thick walls."

"I see God in my soul, my king. Didn't I tell you that he is the source of all light that is around us, that he is inside each one of us? He is our creator and our lord."

"Does your God see you, Zabiba? Does he see all those who believe in him as you do?"

"Yes, my king. He sees me and sees all who believe in him. He sees us always and everywhere, when we worship him and when we are sincere in our prayers, when we pray for him to grant us his mercy and blessing; then he sees us and hears us. He sees the one who disobeys him too. He sees and hears everything, and some receive punishment while others reward, as they deserve."

"You mean your God can hear you too?"

"Yes, our God hears us when we wholeheartedly appeal to him in our prayers."

"Our gods can't hear us until we come close to the place where they dwell. They can hear and see us only when we come into their range of vision, when nothing prevents them from seeing us. That is why they do not see us when we leave the place of worship and can hear us only when we are there. They hear us when we bring them gifts and sacrifices, at least, so we are told by their priests. Through these we receive news about whether or not our gifts had been accepted and whether the god is pleased with us. That is how we know that he has seen and heard us."

"Do you actually have visible gods?"

"Yes, Zabiba, you can see them."

"And even touch?"

"That's right, you can even touch them."

"And do they answer you?"

"Yes, they answer as I have already told you."

"So how is it that they answer you?"

"They answer us when they are pleased with what we do, for instance, when we bring them sacrifices. The more sacrifices one brings to the god, the more pleased that god is."

"And does everyone who believes in a god need to have him, my lord?"

"Yes."

"So, the king has his god. And probably the courtiers, emirs, large tradesmen, and merchants all have their gods. Then it looks to me like your god is not for all people, my king."

"Everyone who wants to and who can afford to do it makes his own god according to his means."

"What means are you talking about?"

"Material means, of course. That is why our gods all differ in size, in what they are made out of, and in how rich their dwelling places are."

"So, then your gods are material, my king?"

"What do you mean, Zabiba?"

"I mean that you can see and touch them."

"Yes, you can see and touch them, like I said."

"So, that means that they are made of matter."

"That's right, that's what they are."

"In that case why are their gifts to you not material so that you can touch them? Why do they not reimburse you for your gifts and sacrifices?"

"What do you mean to say by that, Zabiba?"

"Why don't they pay you back in the same way? You give, they pay."

"But that is how merchants operate, not gods. We do not bring our gifts in hope of getting something back, we..." the king stopped himself.

It was obvious that the king wanted to say that even if they weren't bringing the gifts, the gods would give the people what they asked for, but he suddenly realized that wasn't at all the case, and stopped.

Zabiba smiled and said to herself, "You bring gifts to them and they give you nothing back. They receive and don't return."

Then she said to the king, "So, your gods give to you only when you bring them gifts. And they don't give the same to everyone, but only according to the amount of gifts and sacrifices each man brings, correct? That means that the value of your gods depends on your position and the quantity of your possessions. It turns out that the greatness of the gods themselves differ depending on the position and wealth of their worshippers and the value of the gifts they can afford. And since different people bring gifts of different values, all are not equal before the gods, and even the gods themselves are not equal among each other."

"That is right."

Zabiba said, "It looks like your gifts are material, but your returns are questionable."

The king asked, "Could you repeat that last phrase, please?"

"I said that your sacrifices are material, but whether or not you get anything back should be questioned, my king."

"Yes, that is how it is with our gods."

"Will you promise me mercy, my king?"

"You are my beloved and the very beat of my heart. You know how I treat you. You will always have my protection, Zabiba."

"I want to say something now, not to criticize you, my king, but because of my respect for you and for the abilities of your mind, which could serve the people greatly. Oh, if your mind could only free itself from its chains, if it could throw off the burden under which it groans, the burden of concern with the gods, questions of power, and conspiracies! I am ready to serve you and, therefore, to serve my people as well."

The king interrupted her and said, "Don't tell me that my mind could serve the people, but rather say that I can bless my subjects, for I am the lord of my people, and not their servant."

"Forgive me, my king. Of course, you are the lord of your people, and not its servant."

"No, I can *never* be a servant, Zabiba."

"I beg your forgiveness, my king, and ask for you patience. I do not mean to say that the one who serves the people serves each representative separately, as do those who are hired to wait and serve in exchange for pay. I mean that you, as the leader of the people, on the basis of strict principles, intervene for the interests of the people by protecting the borders of our kingdom, multiplying its riches, preserving high ideals, and bringing all that is noble and useful to the life of the people. You take care of the people who put the power into your hands, so that you could serve their principles. That is how one should correctly understand service to the people."

The king said, "Isn't the presence of foreign powers on the land of the state contradictory to noble ideals? Don't you see that many kings around us invited foreigners? Even now they are still in their lands. Don't you think that it casts a shadow on them and their nations?"

"Yes, my great king. Truly, foreign presence, whether by invasion or invitation, influences the worldview and traditions of the people. And it destroys the freedom of the will of its king, contradicting the notion of a free state, and the sons of that country are not free in it."

"Those kings say that it is better that way."

"What is better, my king?"

"They say that it is better for the foreigners to come to their land, even when the freedom of these rulers is limited so that they are not then free to contradict the desires and plans of the foreigners."

"And explain to me how is that better, my king?"

"So that the rulers don't have to serve the people, which they would have to do if their state was freed from the foreigners."

"But in that case they are serving the foreigners, my king."

"Perhaps, but they say that one day, all the foreigners, together with their armies, will leave and go where they came from. They will leave and then the rulers will be both free and unburdened by a tie with their people. They will be completely free instead of becoming the servants of the people. Then they will not be serving the foreigners because the foreigners will be far away at that point. Doesn't that make sense, Zabiba?"

"No, my king, everything is not as simple as you say, even if we were to agree with some elements of your reasoning for the discussion's sake."

"How is that, Zabiba?"

"It's easy to find people who are ready to serve foreigners, thinking that their needs and security will be fulfilled, but if one does serve them, he will not only be a servant, but also a prisoner. And a shameful prisoner at that, for he surrendered to the enemy of his nation without fighting, as is proper. He will have broken neither a spear, nor a sword, nor a bow. He will be in servitude with no pay, as those who wait in the houses and shops, or something like that. He will do the kind of work which is not even close to being a lawful vocation. There is a great difference between a king and a common man. If a common man is hired by a contract, he has the right to break the contract or to change it if there is no worthy work for him. But the king, if he serves under foreigners, cannot do that. And the people will be against the king, until they finally lose their trust in him. If the king reasons and acts like this, the people will never unite under his leadership and will never forgive him. But people will allow much even to a novice ruler if he attempts to make his people powerful, if he stands up for their interests and independence, even if makes mistakes along the way. The people will allow him to begin again and to correct those mistakes. But the people will not forgive the one who betrays his people. The people will forgive anything of the one who accepts the will of the people and does not go against it, who is ready to offer significant sacrifices, sacrificing even the crown. But the one who accepted conditions placed upon him by the foreigners, humiliating the honor of the people and forgetting about what a strong state is, that person will never be forgiven by the people; against him the people will revolt. Then that king or ruler will experience loneliness in its fullest sense, and the one who is lonely knows what abandonment means and trembles from fear. Your position won't be any better, my king, if you will become like those kings around us. You will be in the fist of a foreigner and will jump to the movements of his fingers. You will serve him in everything, do whatever he demands from you, whether you like it or not. You will lose the sweet taste of what it means to serve the people and to be their lord or, if you allow, their lord and servant. If you submit to foreign powers you will never become a lord again. You will become a miserable servant and not the kind of servant who performs good deeds. So instead of fawning before foreigners, isn't it better to be a servant and lord of your people?"

"Yes, but it is better to be a *lord* and servant of the people, Zabiba."

Zabiba got up, embraced the king with both of her hands and without asking for his permission, kissed him on the forehead. Such is the kings' custom, that if a common woman wants to kiss the king, she needs to ask his permission first, and he has the right to allow or decline. However, if the king wants to kiss any woman from the people, he has no need to ask anybody permission.

\*\*\*

The king said, "I want to look into the past again, and say that back when I visited you in the hut near the house of the miserable Hiskil and when you came to my palace, I could sense in your words an experience of the common people and a deep understanding of the concerns of power. Tell me, where and how did you learn about all this?"

"Is the answer to this question really important to you, my king? Do I have to tell you?"

The king was surprised that Zabiba was not eager to answer and wanted to know the secret of her reluctance even more. He said, "Aren't clarity and equality the elements on which any relationship stands?"

Zabiba answered, "Yes, my king."

"Isn't equality between lovers necessary, Zabiba?"

Saying that, the king borrowed something Zabiba herself used to say, as if to remind her of her own feelings and therefore encourage her to answer his question."

Zabiba said, "Yes, my king, I have said that to you before."

"Would you want for yourself what you do not wish for others?"

"God forbid me from doing that, my king! That would be selfish and nobody would trust me after that."

"Then answer my question."

"As you wish, my lord."

Zabiba thought to herself, "How wonderful it is that the king is becoming more in tune to the common people's ways of equality and justice." She was satisfied to see the king's opinions gradually conforming to her own as their relationship progressed. Zabiba's greatest dream was to have an influence on the establishment of a strong kingdom based on truth and justice. All her life, she dreamt of a nation where equality would flourish and where the emirs could not enslave the weak or common people. Now, thanks be to Allah, all her dreams were coming true, for she had become an influential person who could prepare the king to make the necessary decisions for a radical change. At the same time, she felt helpless in her new love for the king. How could she ever communicate her great love for him when she was legally bound to her husband? How could she influence the king to adopt principles of truth and faithfulness when she herself was breaking these principles? A storm of mixed feelings raged in her heart. Feelings of joy and happiness at seeing part of her dream come true and feelings of pain and brokenness at the reality that she could never unite her soul and body with her king. Only the future would reveal the mysterious destiny that awaited her, the king, and the kingdom.

"On the other hand, the king found himself becoming increasingly attracted to and more deeply in love with Zabiba. Though he knew the risk of this new relationship, he found himself drawn to her speech and attached to her beauty. He was well aware that what she had in her mind and in the curves of her body was influencing him until he was powerless to resist it. The king had had a myriad of relationships with other women, but he had never known anyone like Zabiba, who was a combination of beauty, innocence, and intelligence. In his eyes, she surpassed all others. Of course, the new romance between Zabiba and the king roused the jealousy of the queen and the other women of the palace. Also, the king's brothers who wanted the throne for themselves decided that they should strike while the king was distracted by his new love. They were unaware of Zabiba's keen intuition of their evil schemes. They also failed to realize that Zabiba's intelligence was leading the king to a reformation that would reach the core of the palace and its inhabitants. The incidents were rapidly leading to a climax. How capable was Zabiba of leading the king toward reformation? Would the king respond? Would she be too late to stop the conspirators? How would Zabiba's relationship to the king end? Many questions raged in Zabiba's mind. Though hindered from finding any answers, she was determined to continue her journey to her destiny."

It was still obvious that she would prefer not to answer, but he did not release her from his request.

"I have been telling you about things related to the people, about their principles and feelings, their way of thinking, and about accepting what the people accept and rejecting what they reject."

And she added to her remark about rejecting what people reject, "But I cannot tell you the opinion of the whole people. I can only represent the opinion of the majority."

"And why can't you express the position of all people? Have I not promised you equality in our conversation?"

"Yes, you promised that, my king, but I did not want to tell you about this difficult issue until I knew you would be ready to carry the weight of it. I wanted to wait, so that it would not be too hard for you to hear what it is that the people don't accept."

"So you did that by your own volition and not because I did not allow you freedom to speak, didn't you?"

"Yes, my king, because of my own volition, because I can sense you very well."

"How is that, Zabiba?"

"Life has taught me, as it did all other common people, to accept things I do not wish to accept if another has the authority to impose his will on me. This I am taught to do and so are all other common people taught to do from the very beginning of our lives. But you are not used to doing so, because the decisions of your life are made by you and accomplished by others. They are presented in such a way that neither the common people nor those who surround you can disobey your decisions. You will not give up your way, even when it does not receive the people's support, or if the people would not accept it if they had a right to reject it. That is why you need relationships on a very different level. You need to understand what responsibility is. That is why I tried not to tell you about this, until it was the right time; for you allowed me to represent the conscience of the people. I know everything that the people accept and reject. According to my plan, I will tell you everything, in its time."

"But don't I have to know everything in order to make a final decision, Zabiba? Don't I need to have a complete clarity in everything, or at least in the most essential aspects? Don't I have to know all about the people as the people know all about me, so that I could accept them just as they are, and so that they would accept me the way I am?"

"Yes, my king, but everything has its timing, and the deep starts at the shoreline. People are not always ready and not everyone can jump into the deep and struggle against the strong current. That is why they swim close to the shore for a while. Nobody could dive into the deepest part if he had not first swum to it, and if he were not ready for it mentally and in a practical way."

"That is true, Zabiba. So you will tell me all about the life of the people later, won't you?"

"Yes, my king, both the good and the bad."

"Is there anything bad in the life of the people that resembles what happens in the corridors of the king's palace and in his chambers?"

"Yes, my great king, there is, but there also isn't."

"How is that, Zabiba?"

"There are bad things in the life of the people. However, the vices of the people are unlike those in the corridors of the king's palaces. It is bad that the people have unworthy desires, poor behavior, and greed."

"No, the people are as greedy as kings then?"

"The people are not greedy, my king, but there are greedy people among them. Everyone is greedy in his own way."

"What else?"

"What is black and white has been confused by the people to the point they cannot distinguish between them unless they decide to."

"Listen to me, Zabiba, it seems that I am in the same position as a man who escapes from the heat of the sun only to jump into the flames of a fire."

"Not quite, my king. Conspiracies, power struggles, intrigues and things of this sort which appear in kings' palaces or even in the kings' attitudes toward the people and its problems, are not born out of defects of conscience, lack of clarity, poor education or inadequate training. Other things settled in those peoples' souls, and that is why the illness is progressing. The one who can distinguish the unworthy qualities in the people, which we just mentioned, will be capable of eliminating them by means of conscience, clarity, training, faith, and by making just laws which are decisively enforced."

"Are you sure people want decisiveness from their leader, Zabiba?"

"Yes, my great king, people right now need decisiveness, so that good people find protection in it and so that those who are still weak in their souls fear it."

"I understand you. But let's go back to my question. How could you learn about power and administration so much—you, as a common woman, and as I have known you from the moment we met?"

"I would not say 'known,' my king, for you do not know much about me."

"How is that possible, Zabiba?"

"That's how women are. They do not parade all of their qualities for everyone to see. Such is a female character and so a woman behaves in her relationship with a man. And since you have not asked me this question before, I did not want to tell you what I am about to tell you now. However, I want to ask you something."

"Ask, Zabiba. What is your desire?"

"May we relax for a while, so that I can smell your aroma and kiss you?"

The king smiled and said, "Allah be my witness, I was just going to ask that of you, my beloved Zabiba. But the people should come before the kings because they are closer to life. Isn't that what you were going to say, Zabiba?"

"I would have said it if you did not say it yourself."

They enjoyed the break and then returned to their conversation.

The king said, "I am ready to listen to you, Zabiba."

"And I am ready, and I fully intend to serve my king."

The king said, "You have my attention, Zabiba"

Zabiba answered as if she had just returned from the world of dreams and had suddenly woken up, "Oh, yes, my king, I am ready."

And she said, slightly embarrassed, "Our house stood, as you know, very close, in fact almost adjoining the house of Hiskil, and at first he wanted to tear it down because its appearance marred the view from his gorgeous palace. The house was made out of clay, covered with branches and reeds, and then coated with clay again. It was made simply from cheap materials, but my father wanted to make it cozy inside. He used plaster which was left over from the building of the palace and covered the inside walls of the house with it. He also inserted some windows so that the sunlight could come in. He found the windows in the rubble which was left after Hiskil's workers destroyed an old house nearby. So we lived in this house, my father and I, until I got married and then we all began to live together."

Zabiba stopped for a moment and thought to herself, "Should I tell the king everything about my relationship with my husband and my feelings toward him?"

Then she answered herself, "Rightly do the wise say that a woman who tells another man about her struggles in her relationship with her husband tries to attract him or at least sends him that message. No, I will not tell him about this."

Then she looked into her soul again and asked it, "But isn't the king over all that we do and we can tell him everything we want, when we complain about something that gives us no peace? How can he help me, if he is not convinced that I am right? And how will he know if I am right if he does not know the whole story?"

And she continued already out loud, "My husband treated me as if he had acquired me to satisfy his sexual needs, as if he were a ram among a herd of sheep and I were just one of them. He dragged me to bed without even trying to prepare me. He never asked for my permission, and my father was also in a difficult position, often sleeping outside because he felt very uncomfortable. My father came into the house only out of necessity, or when he knew that my husband was away. Imagine, my great king, he would ask me to add a new victory to his record. 'How many times did we do it today, Zabiba? How many times more till we do our norm?' So he would ask me, and so he would treat me, never asking if I wanted to or not. He never tried to express any human feelings to the one he was using, and he thought of everything he did as if it were only meant for his pleasure. And when at times, I asked him about it, he told me that he wanted to show me how much he loved me by how many times we were in bed, and that it was the only way he could express his attraction to me. Perhaps, in his mind, he was wondering if he should say that this is how I was paying off my father's debt for the money he took for me."

"Did you have a child?"

"No."

The king smiled and she knew that he was trying to say, "How could it happen that you did not have children if you both are young and did what you just told me about?"

Zabiba said, "In the beginning of our life together, I got pregnant with a daughter, but I had a miscarriage because he kicked me in the belly when dragging me to bed. He would often beat me very cruelly. After that, we did not have anymore children. And I thank Allah that it was so."

"How can you say that, Zabiba? Isn't giving birth to a child not the calling of those who live this life?"

"Yes, it is, but not everyone is capable of fulfilling it."

"Yet it is a part of the calling of those who are able to do it."

"That's right, my king, but besides ability, one also needs desire to do it."

"I agree, Zabiba, it is hard to imagine someone being capable of doing it if he has no desire to do it."

"In any case," said Zabiba, "my husband was counting how many times he was in bed with me but he could not awake my womb or my soul, so that I could bear a child again. He did it methodically as one who rapes a woman against her will.

"And one should respect the desires of a woman, for sometimes her desire is necessary to bear a child, my king. Without that desire, she may never have children again."

"A woman's desire is important because it is hard to imagine what would happen without it. Don't women create half of our society? If they begin to hate the other half of society, the rudder of the ship will break. What will happen if they begin to avoid the other part of society, while having such a strong impact on it?"

"We've come to the same conclusion again. Is it not because we are capable of understanding each other and yearn for it?"

"Yes, Zabiba, that is exactly how we are right now. We have common desires and common abilities and also we have equality. Both parts feel it, even though one of us is a king and the other is from the people. We both desire to agree with each other and not disagree."

The king smiled and added, "Except for some cases."

"Yes, my great king, the one for whom I would give my very soul! You've started talking almost as heartily as the people do."

"After all this you still say 'almost?'"

"Yes, my king, one needs to take into account the remaining effects of the state in which you lived before these radical changes occurred in you. Isn't the title of a king different from the status of a common man? That is why I say 'almost.' The king should not forget his title, because he must carry the burden that comes with it. Also, the people should not forget its responsibility before the government to carry its burden, and in addition, should not worry about things which it is not supposed to worry about.

"But back to my story. Hiskil would have large banquets, to which he invited many people, every day after dawn. So emirs, ministers, noblemen, rich merchants and large scale pimps all came to his parties, both women and men."

"Do pimps have their own hierarchy, like government or royal family?"

"Yes, my king, each has his own position depending on the realm of his influence, his specialty. There are large, small and medium scale pimps."

"Were they invited on equal basis with the others?"

"Yes, my king, almost equal."

"And again you said 'almost.' I'm beginning to hate that word."

"Yes, my lord, because the one who builds relationships with another not by attempting to achieve commonality, but through a pimp, is no better than the pimp himself and of the same worth as him. But naturally, the nobility treats them as if they were equals, because if the pimp is not pleased, his *client* will not get what he wants."

"Zabiba, you put a person in the position of a thing, when you said 'what.'"

"Yes, my lord. Because the one who offers herself and her beauty in such a way ceases being human."

Then she continued, "They danced there, drank wine till they were bombed, and everybody did what they wanted without asking permission. What I mean is, what they wanted in matters which require desire or at least no unwillingness. Imagine, my king, how on some nights when the moon was bright, they played a game called "tearing in the woods." The game was played like this: Everybody would run out of the palace into the garden and yard, and then the men would try to take the women. Any woman could be "torn apart" by any man and they had no previous agreement. A woman could defend herself using only her hands, while the man would try to take her, till he overcame her by force. Or they would pretend to defend themselves. Then they would all go back to the palace to boast about what curious things had taken place when they played the game, during "tearing." And that cursed Hiskil was the one who invented and hosted all these games."

"And what about you, Zabiba?" asked the king.

"What do you think I did, my king?" said Zabiba in reply.

"I think only the best of you. You are a very virtuous and noble person, Zabiba, but you were among those people that you are telling me about."

"Yes, my king, that kind of environment attracts those who cannot resist its temptations, but it cannot overpower strong people, who gain strength from within themselves. I was the very Zabiba you imagine and the way you want to see me, the daughter of the people and its conscience. I would leave as soon as they started their disgusting games, but I would witness them from a distance. The women who would not agree to participate, their husbands would divorce them, in fear of being spurned by Hiskil and his gang. And if a man did not want to make his wives go out, Hiskil and his company would beat him until he submitted. And all of them would eventually submit, except for one, my husband. I do not know why they would let him play in these games even though he did not take me with him and did not even dare to ask.

"I had a friend who was a server there. I so much wanted to see the life of those people, to find out what they think about and what they are like. I knew everything about my life, so I wanted to find out about the lives of others. My friend and I decided that I would dress as a server like she, who would be waiting on Hiskil's guests in the palace and would do what servers do, bringing the jugs with wine and goblets, pouring wine in the goblets when guests asked, and serving it to them. They treated me nicely and sometimes even invited me to play in their games of chance."

Zabiba could see that the king was surprised, thinking that she would play their games and said, "No, my king, my principles do not allow duplicity. When I would sit down with them, my principles did not suffer from that. But I never played their games, and most of all, I would never allow any of them whose head was spinning because of too much wine make me drink it."

The king said, "They would let you sit with them, Zabiba?"

"Yes, and sometimes they tried to take me, but with no luck."

She said it as if to brag before the king and added, "You should have seen them! Those emirs, ministers, and merchants would kiss my feet, the feet of Zabiba, the daughter of the people. They were hoping I would submit to what they wanted, but I would proudly decline."

Zabiba was saying all of this, forgetting whom she was talking to.

"But doesn't the fact that they would invite you to sit with them and would try to win your favor show that they forgot about their positions and titles with you?"

"No, my king, they wanted to conquer the people by doing it to me, because they could not do it to the people before."

"Are you sure that it was as you say it was?"

"My king, a person who, after erasing all social boundaries and differences in his soul and conscience, speaks with people as his mind and conscience command, differs from a person who speaks with common people from time to time, led by sudden urges of his soul. That is why you, my king, as well as your people, need to understand that the difference is in the attitude. If somebody truly means well for the people, no conditions, events, or shifts of mood can change his attitude. If his attitude is insincere, this lie will become obvious right away. True union with the people expresses itself in the unity of will and faith. If one only imitates good intentions, that is transparent and very easy to see through. If the person means well, the union is constant. If the person is putting on an act, unity is visible only from time to time, and becomes a strategy, not an expression of human will and desire. That is why their ingratiation before me did not at all mean that they had rejected their way of thinking and their ideals for my sake. All that was only intended to conquer me."

"And what did you do, Zabiba?"

"I was like the one who crosses a plowed field in a dark night, whose only light is her heart."

"Good, Zabiba! Indeed, the light in us is the true light, which will neither allow the eye, nor the soul, nor the heart to err."

"Yes, my king, the one for whom I would give my very soul. Say these things so that all the people in the whole world can hear you. Speak like the people speak, so that you can become close to us, and so that you do not differ from us in anything except in what is demanded by your status, which you only hold for our sake."

"Wonderful, Zabiba! If you had not added 'for our sake' after 'status,' I would definitely be angry with you."

"But how could I bear the displeasure of my beloved and my lord?"

And they both burst out laughing.

***

The hadjib of the palace came in and told the king that several emirs were asking for his audience.

The king asked, "Who is among them?"

The hadjib started listing their names.

The king listened to his report but then ordered him to leave, saying that he would ask for him when he was ready.

The hadjib left.

The king's decision was absolutely right. Even though there was nothing to make him doubt the emirs' intentions, the king found out before seeing them that this meeting was part of a conspiracy directed against him and Zabiba. Among the demands that they were going to place before him was that Zabiba never be allowed to come to the palace again (her visits were almost daily now, and she had become the king's consultant, especially in the questions concerned with the people and its problems).

Zabiba was able to continue her story. "I saw how the more prosperous merchants were plotting against less fortunate tradesmen; and how some groups were attacking other groups; how every merchant competes with the others as they try to outdo each other in profit and in deceit. And just as the merchants and pimps compete among themselves, emirs also compete over the king. Over you, my great king! And when the question of who will become the next heir arises, they separate from all others and aim conspiracies against each other. It was hard for me to watch when two emirs lost in a gamble and Hiskil told them to sell their armor to a merchant who came from the country Alam, just so that they could keep playing. One of them sold his sword and the other sold his full armor. And so did many of them. They sold their weapons and horses to the merchant from Alam, to Hiskil himself, or to anybody else who came there from far away. I wanted to ask them at that moment where they would get armor if they needed to fight. But in my soul I already had an answer to this question, 'The one who could buy their weapons and armor to provide funds for gambling could also buy emirs themselves for the assistance he would be willing to provide in their conspiracies. He would supply them with the weapons to kill you and then he would take them back.'"

"Did all the players do that?"

"Yes, my king, each of them were ready to sell even their own wives, which they partially already did by bringing them to such places where men gamble and drink wine."

"How is that, Zabiba?"

"If a husband allows his wife to be where men gamble and drink, it means that he is prepared not to feel jealous of his wife when she is exposed to the glances of other men, and at times, to their base advances. Shouldn't a man protect his wife from the solicitation of other men and monitor her behavior? Couldn't a wife easily be seduced if her husband were not protective of her? Alas, all emirs, merchants and noblemen who were invited there did not protect their wives. Hiskil explained to those who were reluctant to do it that they had no place among them. He told them that since they were not going to do what Hiskil wanted, they were old-fashioned, immature, and unworthy to rise to his level. That situation is terrible, but it is even worse that we see this evil differently. Do you know, my king, that they would bring into their houses fair skinned, blue eyed people who came from distant lands, but they did not let in others who had much more right to be there? After that, is anything sacred for them? After all that, do they have even a notion about what is pure? After that, do they have anything left from the morality which ties them to our people and to all other peoples around us? Do they have anything left at all? Could that be possible, my king? Is it possible?"

Zabiba even started crying, so miserable were those whom she was talking about. But she wiped her tears and kept talking, while the king helped to calm her.

"While I was among them I learned everything I needed, my king. I learned to do everything which does not correspond to their ways, behavior, and thinking because I rejected their philosophy and behavior consciously and prudently, when my soul convulsed from what I was seeing. I realized on what we must stand, when my conscience, filled with deep faith and the glorious role of the people, revealed to me what the interests and goals of the people were."

"How wonderful, Zabiba!" said the king.

But before he had a chance to remind her that it was their usual time to part, Zabiba said, "And now that you know everything, would it burden the king to give me my wish?"

"Wish away, Zabiba."

"Forgive me, my king. I thank you for your mercy and compassion."

"You are speaking to me as if you are seeing me for the first time!"

"No, my king, this is a request of a subject to the king, and in that case, tact and respect are appropriate. Isn't one of the elements of politeness in keeping close to the rules of propriety, remembering them always, and never forgetting the requirements of elementary politeness?"

"That's right, Zabiba. And the one to whom we appeal will listen to us more attentively and will be prone to help us if we observe the norms of politeness when talking to people. Say what it is that you wanted to say, Zabiba."

"First tell me, now that you have heard my whole story and I told you everything about my husband, do you think I have the right to request a divorce?"

"And what would prevent you if you decide to do so, Zabiba?"

"Nothing except for my weakness."

"You are not weak, Zabiba, you are strong!"

"No, my king, even a hero can be weak before the law."

"What law could prevent you from divorcing your husband?"

"My husband paid the bride-money to my father, who needed money desperately to help him out of a difficult situation. And though my husband was my cousin, blood relationship did not stop him, and he wanted to marry me taking advantage of my father's need for money, which my future husband had plenty of after he wormed his way into Hiskil's gang. I don't even know when and how they met each other. My father suggested that I marry but gave me the right to choose because before that, I had always turned my cousin down when he asked me to marry him. I told him that I would marry him only if he were to leave the company of Hiskil, abandoning their customs and habits. When my father asked me to marry for the last time, I agreed under the conditions that I would remain in the house in which you have visited us, and that he would be living with us in that house. My future husband by that time had adopted all the customs of his lords and partners in games and married several times. Like his friends, he also had concubines. I agreed to marry him under these conditions and he accepted them. What happened after that could hardly be called marriage, more of a business transaction. The worst thing was that my husband treated me as though, by purchasing me, he was destroying my honor. He wanted to crush me, but I resisted with all my strength. For if high principles live in one's soul they give that person the perseverance, patience, and ability to resist. I fought him until I met you.

"And even though the abuse which I received from the husband who constantly beat and humiliated me ended, for easily understood reasons, when you started to visit our house, I, nonetheless, remained his purchase, and I cannot free my neck from his noose until I can be free from the sum of money which he paid for me."

"The money would help you when you make your final decision about your husband?"

"Yes, my king, and here is the main thing. I agreed to this marriage in order to not be a burden to my father who could not support both of us anymore. I have not been happy with my husband even for a moment. However, our separation will have to take place not just because of my desire to do so, but according to the law."

The king said, smiling, "Anything you want."

Then she threw herself at him and embraced him around his shoulders. She kissed his head and forehead; she kissed his hands, but when she wanted to kiss his feet, he lifted her up and would not allow her. Their bodies were so close to each other that they almost touched, and the king kissed her on the forehead.

Zabiba started crying. Her tears dropped on the king's cheek and on his clothes. Then she wiped her tears and said, "May Allah keep you with me and with my people. You by right are the king of our great kingdom."

***

When it was time to depart, Zabiba asked for the king's permission to head home, but the king did not give it. So she began talking about other topics, not what they had been talking about before.

The king asked Zabiba, "How would you describe your love for me, Zabiba?"

"When I say that I love you, my king, the phrase goes all through me before it slips off my tongue. I say it as everyone else does, but the origin of the words, its source, is not the same. Perhaps even the direction of the letters is different when I say 'I love you.' And if you want me to say more, my king, I will tell you that if a person feels as if everything around her, including nature, is being transformed by light, this light comes from no other source but from the rays of her love, which it is as impossible to live without as it is impossible to live without the sun. It means that she loves truly. That is why I felt that I was not mistaken in my love for you, my king, even though I do not worship your ancient gods. I began to love you in my soul, my king, when our relationship started painting the life surrounding us with different colors. After this, shouldn't the soul come out to the forefront? Shouldn't it soar the heights, since it itself is in an elevated state? A human being without a soul is nothing but a bag of bones. Could one pen up his soul or limit its flight? Doesn't Allah alone appoint the soul to where it should find its dwelling?"

"Yes, Zabiba, you are right again. Love that settles in the heart alone, but not in the soul, is prone to being manipulated by things of this world. And the one who is under the influence of those things becomes composed of things. Things receive their value from the level of their influence. That man looks at his beloved in parts. Ultimately he separates from her the eyes, separates her breasts, mind...he separates her body from her and loves the body alone. But if he were to love a person in his wholeness, with his soul and body, character, qualities and behavior, then love would have a different dimension and would embrace all of these aspects, free from the tie to the objects, including the body parts which invoked that love. If love accepts the form and color of things, it means that that love can be influenced. It can be weakened by the hardships and difficulties standing in its way; it can change its direction under the influence of obstacles. But all this cannot sway the soul. That is why, among other reasons, a man needs a distant god who cannot be touched or seen, and who will not be a part of this earth or things in this world. That is why I fell in love with you, Zabiba. In you, I saw the light and the reflection of my own soul. You are my doctor and my medicine."

Zabiba asked, "But why, why did you fall in love with me, my great king?"

"I fell in love with you, Zabiba, so that in you and through you I could love the people. I understood you while I was listening to what you were saying. I understood you while I was watching what you were doing. I could see that you were capable of self-sacrifice and that you espouse everything that you speak about. I understood your God, because you were a living part of the people, and because you believe in his role and love your native land. Through my love for you, I grew to love the people, and after that, I grew to love your God. I grew to love your people, Zabiba, and that is why I grew to love your God. Or perhaps your God gave me my love for you and the people, after I grew to love him.

"I realized that there is no inconsistency in the love of a ruler for his people and his love for God. I realized that the one who does not love people couldn't love the only God, like your Lord, Zabiba. Also, I realized a clear contradiction between our gods and our love for the people, because our gods honor our wishes in accordance with our status and purpose, and they always deal differently with the wishes of the people. That is why after I fell in love with you and grew to love your people, I decided to accept your faith and reject my gods. I decided to destroy my gods to achieve harmony with myself after I fell in love with you with my entire soul. I love you and your people with my whole soul and I will even sacrifice my soul for you. I yearn for your God with my whole soul and beg him for forgiveness and mercy."

When the king uttered the last phrases, tears streamed from his eyes and flowed down his cheeks and mustache. Zabiba jumped up, and also shedding tears, embraced him, kissed him on the forehead, and said, "We praise Allah for his creation, for giving us birth and showing us the way, for what he has prepared for us, and for the glory and happiness that he has given us. I believe in you, O God, the Lord of two worlds."

The king said, "I too, believe."

A moment later, he turned to Zabiba again and said with slight embarrassment, "If you love me the way I am, and since I love you the way I think you are, would you agree to have me for your husband according to the law of your God, Zabiba?"

It was so unexpected that for a moment Zabiba's tongue went numb and happiness overflowed her and tingled her cheeks and lips. But she gained control over herself and said to the king, "It is not in my habits to reject the will of my king, but may my lord allow me to share my opinion with him, if he is willing to hear it."

The king was puzzled and surprised that Zabiba would not want to take advantage of the opportunity that was available to her. To cover his embarrassment, he remembered Zabiba's character and started saying to himself, "Truly, Zabiba is not like everybody else. She has her own opinion about everything. And since I made myself get used to respecting her opinions, or at least to listening to them with respect and good will and judging them with proper attention, I must listen to her now too."

The king spoke again with a smile and some embarrassment, which was as easily recognizable in him as his rage. (Don't kings become angry whenever somebody goes against their will or ruins their plans?) "I am willing to listen to your opinion, Zabiba."

Zabiba started looking for the answers in herself, "Where would the kings of our time gain imagination or where would they get new ideas? Doesn't everything that happens now originate from abroad? What else is left but to obey the foreign influences in submission? Doesn't a guard dog have some space where it can run and bark? The size of the space that the dog gets depends on the kind of place that she is entrusted to guard. When its owner decides to enter and use the domain of her kingdom, he will allot a square meter of land to his dog or put her on a short leash. And if her master decides to act deceitfully with his neighbors, he will make the rope longer, but assure them that they are safely out of the dog's reach. When I think of the dog on the leash, I mean the following: this kind of man is not the owner of his desires. I know that our king is not like other kings, but in the very foundation of how his soul operates, he has something in common with them."

Zabiba stopped contemplating and said, "I fell in love with you, my king, because I was attracted to your innate qualities, though I am in general against kings and against the succession by which the kings come into power. I am especially against the hereditary system, where an heir becomes king whether or not he is capable of reigning, independent of his abilities, character or the people's opinion. My hate for it intensified when I saw with my own eyes how the gatherings and parties at Hiskil's place look, perhaps because of such power and such kings. In your personality, I saw a foundation which would allow you to carry on your shoulders the weight of care for the people if you decided to do that, O my king. But to determine when and how you will decide to do this is my goal, and I promised Allah that I would accomplish it. Striving to achieve it, I fell in love with you because of what I found in you. It would be right if I said that our union surpasses all of my dreams and paints them into vivid colors. I would never have known that these colors even existed if it weren't for our relationship. But here is the problem: our wedding now could destroy the people's opinion of me, and they would think that all of my struggles, all my patience, all the great difficulties which I overcame on my way, were only intended to lead to our wedding, my king, and not for the sake of the people. Besides, you are still the king. I don't think that our people, intimidated by the kings who fawned before foreigners, would trust a king. In our history there have been kings who could be compared to a pearl in a crown, but in our times, where are the kings who would be equal to the kings of the times past?"

Suddenly, Zabiba remembered that the one she was talking to was also a king. Then she said, "Forgive me, my lord, I swear by Allah that I do not put you in the same row as those against whom my arrows are intended. I speak to you as if you were almost like me."

"Once again, you say 'almost,' Zabiba."

"Yes, my king, because you are still the king and I am still called Zabiba. Zabiba, the daughter of the people and the conscience of the people."

"But if we get married, you will be a queen and then our attributes, having united, will achieve equality."

"No, my king, there will be no equality, because even as a queen, I will be in a position subordinate to you and therefore not independent. Then, I will not be able to behave in a way which, ideally, my independence would allow me. In that case, I will lose my freedom. I will change from a daughter of the people whom the king allows to speak her mind and to whom the king gives equality in his conversations with her into a queen, and from one who has acquired freedom as the living conscience of the people into a queen, a mere attachment to the king, constrained by her title and other heavy chains."

"What you are saying, Zabiba, is true in part. Especially concerning the role of the queen. But you would gain great privileges, including the glory which now you do not have."

"Yes, my king, I will gain privileges and yet I will lose my freedom, and with it the privileges that I have right now."

"What privileges, Zabiba?"

"In part it is glory, my king; in part, influence and a special role."

"How is that, Zabiba?"

"My glory comes from the importance of my role, from the name that the people gave me: Zabiba, the daughter of the people and its living conscience. My role consists of representing the people before the king, being its conscience in my conversations with him, being its experience and its mind in my advice to the king. And in addition to this, I am free because I can come to the king, but I am not obliged to come if I do not wish to."

The king said, "You can reject the title of the queen and divorce the king if you so desire."

"No, my king, I cannot venture to do so because I will get used to the royal throne and the royal crown, and to how the people treat me, and to how the guards, maids, and courtiers treat me. When I bask in the rays that stream from the king, then I will change from within, and the outside will have nothing to do but to obey. As for your words that I would be free to leave the king and return to the people, I must warn you, my king, that you will change as soon as I become your wife, and fearing for your reputation, will not give me that freedom then. Kings can reject people, but when people reject a king, the king covers them with the worst curses and instead of blaming himself for what happened, lays all the blame on the people. I also cannot agree to do it for other reasons which I will keep to myself and will tell you some other time. I beg you, my great king, accept my explanations and apologies. Oh, if only my lord would agree to wait with his proposal and let me think everything over.

If only you would choose a better time for it, after the people get to know you better."

"I understand that you reject the form but not the essence of the proposal, Zabiba. You reject the title of a king, but not the man-king. Is the form that important, Zabiba?"

"Yes, my king, the form is important to the degree in which its owner abides by it. And since you abide by this form, its meaning and its influence on your personality and on your soul are equal to the tenacity with which you grasp it. Besides, doesn't form have a great influence on the essence? Form is something that often dictates a person's movements and his behavior. Take clothes, for example. Tell me, does anything change in your behavior and your movements when you dress in royal clothes, put on the royal crown and sit on the throne, or if you put on casual clothes and go to your wife, or if you dress in military attire and put on armor? And since even in those small things there is a huge difference, what could be said of the influence that the form bears on personal qualities and authority, regarding the order of inheritance from king to king as well as many other things?"

\*\*\*

So Zabiba settled it with the king that she would leave her husband, fulfilling her desire to end the duplicity that tortured her. She dashed back and forth between the king's palace and her home, where her husband driven by his lust and desire for power and control tried to prove his mastery over her. Perhaps he was trying to show that he had victory over her, when he subjected her to his will, when he screamed at her, forced her into the bed, or beat her for any insignificant reason. She became the king's beloved, and people spoke of her far beyond the walls of the king's palace. Isn't it normal for people's psychology to either imitate celebrities in everything or to reject them in everything? People try to feel a connection with those who are like them in their characteristics and qualities by adopting their lifestyle or behavior, the products they use or in what they clothe themselves, including hairstyle and beard, the length and width of their mustache, the way they smile and laugh. People want to acquire the same kinds of staff, horses and clothes that celebrities have. The only thing they do not want to have is the ukal.* That is because the ukal in our time has become a symbol of shame, for it is found on the heads of several treacherous kings, their emirs, and associates. If it wasn't for Iraq who saved the ukal because the heart of the nation placed it on its head, the ukal would have become hateful to the Arab soul and the Iraqis would have to say 'God protect us' twice when meeting kings and noblemen who wear ukals on their heads.

*Aren't people prone to imitate celebrities, especially people who lacking essence find comfort in form? Or if they do not imitate the celebrities, do not people reject them with burning hate because they themselves have jealous souls?*

*This the wise old woman said and laughed as if expressing our feelings, but we listened very seriously to everything she was saying about the king and Zabiba, even if all of that was a made-up tale. We were waiting impatiently for the continuation of this peculiar and entertaining story, while the storyteller wanted us to pay attention to her commentary so that we understood the essence and the internal meaning of the story.*

---

* **EDITOR'S NOTE:** Ukal – a rope with which men secure the *kaffiya* (bandana) on their head.

*The old woman continued, "Some lust to have kings' concubines, their wives and daughters. Isn't that very lust, in a way, the beginning of a yearning to acquire something which is not at all possible? In that case, how is lust different from yearning?"*

*With the intent to make all boredom vanish, the old woman addressed the one of the youths among us who was the closest to the age of a man, "If you start thinking of them, at night you will dream that you have taken one of them."*

*And to another of the same age she said, "And you, lad, I see, are deep in your thoughts, already dreaming of some king's daughter!"*

*In reply to her joking, we all laughed. Boys and girls, very anxious to listen again to her exciting story, all gathered around her.*

Zabiba had been riding back home on her gray mare.* She insisted that she would make her journey alone, without any guards to escort her. The king preferred that she take somebody to accompany her, but she had insisted on her decision, so nobody went with her. The king would have ordered somebody to go with her, but, seeing her obstinacy, realized that she would not agree. Fearing that it would upset the king and that he would compel her to do what he wanted, she said before he could convince her otherwise, "It seems to me, my king, that you are in a rush to make me look as if I were one of the princesses with her cortege. By that, you will undermine my authority and influence among the people. One of my main qualities which has a great influence on the people is that I have come close to power and to the one who makes decisions while remaining a part of the people, and not only with my soul and mind but also in my behavior and appearance. I am from their midst

---

* **EDITOR'S NOTE:** This isn't a horse, it's a chameleon!

ZABIBA AND THE KING

and a part of their life. Do you want to deprive me
of my influence, my king? Do you resent me so
much, my king, that you want to sink the ship on
which I sail? Do you want to bridle my freedom, clip
my two wings which allow me to fly between the
trees and to enjoy the beauty of the flowers and
branches leaning over the surface of the river?"

Zabiba said all that to the king rather seriously, but at the same time with slight flirtation,
and the smile never leaving her lips. The king called
that smile "a bee's nectar."

*"And what's a bee's nectar, grandma?"*

*"Honey, of course!"*

*Many of us swallowed and licked our lips as
we suddenly felt a strong craving.*

*The old woman continued.*

The distance between the city and her home
was about five farsachs* long or a little more. On
both sides of the dirt road there was a thick forest
and ditches lined its edges. Many of the kings of
bygone days had built their palaces away from the
cities (unless they wanted to build a new city),
thereby protecting themselves from the people's revolts, because it was hard for common people to
cover the distance between the cities and the palace
by foot. The cities were the usual centers of rebellion, but if the people started riots, the kings,
emirs, and their associates tried to plan their defense so that the rebels would die outside of the
city. Not many from the number of the people were
skillful enough in their usage of weapons and armor to have a chance against the king's guards,
spies and warriors. They often did not even have
such simple things as animals for transportation or
basic weaponry to resist those who were in the pal-

---

* ***EDITOR'S NOTE:*** Farsach - a unit of measurement of distance. Five (5)
farsachs equates to approximately 1.4 miles.

aces. To rebel, people need to assemble using secret tactics of organization. If their moves are not done in secret and if they are not well organized, they will be exposed before they can gain the strength necessary for the attack.

All this was going through Zabiba's head while she traveled home. She fell deep in thought, but suddenly her eye caught a glimpse of some movement among the trees. She spurred her horse to make her gallop, but all of a sudden the road was blocked by a horseman surrounded by other armed men whose faces were covered with masks. Zabiba drew her sword and began to fight bravely, but one of the attackers hit her sword with an iron rod, while two others distracted her with their swords. Her hand went numb and the sword fell to the ground. They dragged Zabiba off the horse and tied her hands behind her back. The leader of the attackers, also in a mask, led her to an opening in the forest while the others followed him at a distance. In the forest, without a single word, he knocked her down on the ground and she realized his intentions. He shut her mouth with a rag, so that nobody could hear her screams. At first Zabiba resisted, but then gave up because of the severity with which he beat her with fists and feet until, bleeding badly, she lost consciousness. Then he raped her, forgetting manliness and honor and with no fear of the shame which would be bestowed on him for what he had done. From that shame, no one among his children or grandchildren or even great-grandchildren will be spared, and he himself will have no place among men. His children will not marry daughters of noblemen or their sons. After that, the thug decided that she was unconscious because she had stopped resisting and was laying motionless with her hands tied. The rag fell out of her mouth while she had been fighting, but he did not notice and fell upon her again. Acting like a wild animal in the attack of desire, he came close to her mouth with his face. Then, Zabiba plunged her teeth into his throat and clenched her teeth as hard as she could, so that a deep wound was left on his neck.

Then the aggressor beat her more viciously than before. Finally, he untied her hands and let her lie there. Zabiba was lying silently until she realized that the night had already fully lowered its cloak. Suddenly she noticed her horse, who was standing with her head bowed over her, sniffing her legs, forehead and hands.

When Zabiba opened her eyes and saw the horse, she smiled at it, even though a great sorrow was pressing on her. She felt herself totally humiliated by what had happened. She smiled to her mare for her faithfulness, even thought it was only the faithfulness of an animal its master. Then she sobbed bitterly, thinking that at times a human being can be much worse than a beast.

That is what the villains had done to Zabiba. They had chosen the one among them who could rip apart her honor, while a wild beast could only rip apart the body. Doesn't a man's behavior depend not only on his mind, but also on the level of his conscience's development, forged in the process of education and training? And even though the primary difference between people and animals is the mind, the mind of a human is not by itself capable of making a man a complete creation especially if his conscience will not be human. The mind is a force, and a force can do both good and evil deeds. The good is certainly possible only as a result of education, learning, and living by examples, while the mind alone cannot guard itself from evil.

From this, it was possible to explain why one man could tear apart another as he had done to Zabiba.

"Even an animal respects a man's desire, if it wants to copulate with him. Doesn't a female bear try to please a herdsman when she drags him into the mountains as it happens in the North of Iraq? She drags him into her den, so that he, obeying her desire, would copulate with her.* Doesn't she bring him nuts, gathering them from the trees or picking them from the bushes? Doesn't she climb into the houses of farmers in order to steal some cheese, nuts, and even raisins, so that she can feed the man and awake in him the desire to have her?

"And this man-beast treated me as less than human when he tore me apart in such a disgusting way. Perhaps this was one of those who tried fruitlessly to have me when Hiskil did not succeed in making me join their nocturnal games."

So was Zabiba saying to herself, "It would have been better if he were to tear me apart with his tusks, if he were to rip my stomach open and kill me! If he were to do so, he would be so much more merciful than when he did what he has done. What will I say to the Lord? Truly, the Lord is merciful and forgives everything, for he sees what a person does according to her will and what is done to her. If I were not afraid that he would torture me on his fire, I would have killed myself. What will I tell the king? Will he even believe my story? And if he will, would he believe that I was resisting this rape? That I did everything I could to stop it? What will I tell myself? Oh, woe, woe is me! I used to trust

---

* **EDITOR'S NOTE:** The Editor assumes that the Author is referring to Russia, whose symbol is the Bear. Though not immediately adjacent, Russia is Iraq's neighbor to the North. Otherwise, this is really demented!

those who were around me, but never will I be the same again.

"But why?" she asked herself again. "Why will I not be the same? What happened was against my will. I resisted it. I tried everything, from the sword to prayer; I reminded the villain about the ideals of manliness and nobility, but none of these helped. I even engaged my teeth. Isn't one a hero if he fights with his teeth if he has to rather than submitting to an armed enemy?"

Then she recalled that she did not submit, but fell unconscious on the battlefield. And when she remembered how she was fighting, her pupils became as large as they could be and she stopped thinking about that, as if she wanted to say, "Here, I have decided; I will tell the king immediately. Isn't it better for a woman who found herself in a similar situation with another man to tell her husband, brother, or beloved everything right away, before he hears about it from others who will make him think badly of her? If I tell everything to the king, perhaps we will find this rabid dog and his pack of criminals. If we find the marks that I left on his neck and his body then we will find out everything."

Then she thought, "But what if the king cannot find the criminal and those with him? What if I tell him about something he did not know and perhaps would not have found out and in that way I will distance him from myself, because I have no proofs of my innocence?"

Then she said to herself, "And what if he finds out? That would mean that our relationship would fall into a chasm and our plans would be threatened."

She decided to tell the king everything as soon as she went home to wash and to change clothes. It would be better if she went to the palace later and allowed the king the opportunity to act on the basis of what she told him, and not on the basis of what the guards would tell him when they saw her like this.

"If I don't tell him, I will bind his hands and give him no opportunity to come up with a solution which he himself will consider necessary and appropriate."

While all these thoughts were swirling in Zabiba's head, the horse was walking down the road by herself, not needing anybody to lead her. She had already gotten used to riding back and forth down this road. What a noble horse! Isn't one truly noble when he perfectly performs his duty in difficult conditions and in hard times? That is one of the main differences between a noble person and an ignoble person.

The mare was heading toward Zabiba's house, but Zabiba had been just deprived of the most precious thing that a woman could have. There was nothing else left to be afraid of, except for her own soul. Who knew what would trouble her soul after everything that had happened. Suddenly, Zabiba felt a terrible loneliness, as if she were covered by a dark cloud. A black and deep loneliness was in her very soul. And she knew the reasons for it. She desired revenge and at the same time feared for the loss of her love. So far, everything that had happened between the king and her had happened according to what they both decided, and she had become used to this situation.

"And now that such a change had happened, something very different would appear before the king. I will stand before him and he will know that I submitted to another man's will, that I was raped. And the fact that I was raped, that I submitted to the mercy of the villains, will become a reason for the king not to want me anymore. The king is used to arguing with me about serious matters; he knows how to extract wise thoughts even in what he calls cavils, when I try to express my opinion tactfully after he has expressed his. He is used to my trying to contradict him even when I see that his opinion is the wisest there is. I act so, because I have the role of the people's conscience, and the people's opinion often contradicts the opinion of the king, and the conscience of the king and of the people do not melt into one whole. He is used to my arguments, and he fell in love with me for that, even though his face was often angry. He does not want to see me surrender. If he sees that even with high ideals, I have been defeated, he will be surprised; he won't bear it and will decide he is tired of me."

Now, Zabiba felt the desire to avenge herself on the rapists more than anything.

"Revenge may be a cure for the wounds of the soul. Revenge is the knowledge of the truth and the desire to settle the score with the least number of losses."

So spoke Zabiba to herself.

And yet in her soul, the feeling of loneliness grew larger, as if a carnivorous beast was tearing her insides, ripping her stomach, her veins, and even her breasts. Didn't the carnivorous brute that attacked her tear them apart, as if to expose her to the king like that? Their gang was not capable of throwing shame on the king directly, even if they really wanted to. So why not throw shame on the king by humiliating his beloved? By taking her and destroying her from the inside, by making her an outcast among the surrounding peoples. A loss of the beloved by the one who loves is a different side of love. Perhaps that is what the villains intended when they dared to do this, but how could they find the one among themselves who would be the most brutal of them all? How did they know that this one would do to her what he did, even if she resisted him? Perhaps it was a soldier who for some reason ran from the battlefield, and then decided to take revenge on the one whom he considered his enemy, in order to heal some inadequacy in himself. Or maybe it was a spy, from whom, because of his own mistake, a wanted criminal had escaped. Or it was a trader of women who sells them to the noblemen while he cannot have any of them for himself, and therefore he developed a hate for all women. Perhaps in the name of all the ill and impotent, he decided to do this evil to the one that had become the symbol of all women before the king.

Then Zabiba said, "A soldier could not have done this because he remembers that his main duty is to protect his country not to destroy it. And the one who lays down his life for the work of protecting his country, so that his friends are proud of him and his enemies indignant, could not do such a thing. The same is true about spies, though we often think badly of them due to our daily encounters. There is a conflict between the one who thinks it his duty to obey the law and the one who thinks that the law interferes with his personal freedom. A secret agent could not do this, because it is a criminal act which was done to me against the law, and the duty of a law enforcement agent is not only to respect the law, but also to make others respect it. Whoever did this would not have done it in such an evil and lustful way unless he had a personal desire to harm me."

And suddenly, she felt as if sharp claws pierced her heart and drew blood from it. But she could not simply explain it away by the condition that she was in after what had happened.

Her husband thought that Zabiba would return to the palace to tell the king about what had happened to her and did not even imagine that she would come home. Zabiba tied the horse near the house, and because she was in such a humiliated state, she approached the house very quietly. Not wanting to speak to anyone, Zabiba peered through a crack in the door only to see her husband half naked as he washed off some blood which flowed from his neck and other parts of his body.

Now that she realized that it was her husband who had raped her, and that it was he who had attacked her with a gang of thugs, new thoughts immediately entered her mind, not the same that she had previously. Now she understood this conspiracy and she knew why it was she who was targeted and not the king. The one who cannot overcome the master, will try to overcome his servant.

"But what made this asshole* (referring to her husband) go for this cowardly and base act? While Hiskil and the gangs of emirs, pimps, and merchants who completely seared their conscience at least had their goal, what made him do this? Don't those who are in power have the cruelest attitude towards virtue and human dignity?

"He is a coward. That's for sure. But that he was also a bastard, I could not presuppose. But don't we judge a person by his deeds? Didn't he try to imitate the king? Or maybe he decided that since he could not be a king, he would be *like* a king if he had the king's beloved? Isn't there a difference, asshole* (about her husband again), between conquering one's desire and rape?"

Then she thought to herself, "The one who cannot think of anything new to please his wife, wouldn't he think that it is enough to rape her to satisfy himself? It is not any better than treating a

---

* *EDITOR'S NOTE:* Asshole –translates literally as "rotten."

festering wound by infecting it again and again. Be you cursed, vile infidel!"

She disgustedly spit on the ground, making noise by the door, so that he did not think that she had seen everything. That would complicate the matter and would make him react differently from the way she wanted him to, and she did not want to reveal anything to him yet.

"Doesn't a change in goals, timing, or choice of resources require additional efforts and time to think? Doesn't a man at times lose a battle because he hastily made changes which were not carefully thought out?"

Thinking so to herself, Zabiba opened the door and walked into the house.

She gave her hateful husband an opportunity to put on clothes and to tie his kaffiya around his head. He started wrapping his throat also, explaining that he had strained his neck. Having decided that Zabiba believed him, he would come up with some excuse every time she got close to him. He was trying to make sure that she did not see his neck and avoided her very carefully. Zabiba, on the other hand, kept showing her interest in what it was that he had there, and she did it so that he started suspecting that she knew.

As to her appearance, he asked her about everything, as if he knew nothing, and made a sad face while Zabiba told him everything in detail, watching his eyes carefully to see his reaction. He then started behaving as if an ifrit* possessed him and wanted to throw him on the ground, break all of his bones, and chase his soul out of him.

Zabiba enjoyed the torture, and she did it with much pleasure. Isn't a woman's desire for revenge much stronger that that of a man? And if she

---

* *EDITOR'S NOTE:* Ifrit - an evil spirit, demon.

finds a way to harm the one she hates, she will make him suffer enough of her tortures and give him a taste of the most bitter defeat. Many men, especially those who have principles, do not yearn for revenge purposely, though it becomes an element of a fight at times. In the case of women, however; if a woman's heart bleeds or if somebody has overcome her, her revenge gains a rather vicious goal, which brings her great pleasure. Probably if given the chance, women would eat alive those who brought them suffering. Don't you know how Hinda, the daughter of Utbah, feasted on the liver of Hamza, may Allah be pleased by him, as a revenge for killing her father, brother and uncle in a battle?*

Zabiba's husband tried to cover up the truth about what had happened and she repeatedly asked him about how he had injured his neck. Her husband, instead of going into an angry rage and threatening to take revenge on the one who had tortured her, reminded Zabiba of a dog which had eaten something in her master's house which was not intended for her or by mistake had bitten the master himself, and been kicked out of the house. The tail of this dog was hanging between her legs and her whole appearance, all her movements and behavior spoke of the extreme level of guilt and humiliation.

And though we are comparing Zabiba's husband to a misbehaving dog, a dog, out of gratitude to her master, would never betray him. On the other hand, Zabiba's husband acted deceitfully against her, and so calling him a dog is too kind. At least one could use the skin of a dog if one washed

---

* **EDITOR'S NOTE:** You can read more about this story at http://www.islamicvoice.com/july.98/child.htm. Look under "Champion of the Prophet (Phub): Hazrath Hamza."

it and processed it, but there was so much filth in her husband's skin that one could not touch it without soiling oneself, even if it were washed by all the waters of the Tigris.

Zabiba cleaned herself up and put on fresh clothes. She put on her sword and came out on her white horse. She hurried up, noticing that the sun could be coming up before she reached the outer walls of the palace. There were many soldiers at the gates and her appearance could arouse many questions and much talk which could not be contained within the walls of the palace. Gossip spreads quickly among the servants and from them, all other people will eventually know about everything. Isn't it enough for servants to simply eavesdrop in order to know what the kings say, think, and do? And don't the tongues of kings' concubines become a herald of their master's demeanor and health? It is better not to be late coming into the palace. The dusk will help me hide the scratches on my face which I got in the fight with this rabid dog.

Zabiba finally reached the palace and, as usual, headed to the king's private chamber. Without asking permission, she came into his bedroom and saw that he was expecting her already—the chief of the guards having reported her arrival to him as soon as he received word from the guards of the external gates.

The king had not yet had time to dress, but he was up and had washed his face in his routine of preparation for her visit. Many thoughts and guesses swirled in his head, and already anxious, he asked himself, "Why am I so worried? They just informed me that it was she and not anybody else that was coming to me, and probably in good health too. I have nothing to worry about. Didn't she ride here from home on her horse? The one who makes a journey between her home and the palace on a horse this early in the day must be feeling good. But why this early of a visit?"

The king had given her permission to come to the palace whenever she wanted, no matter what time it was, and not as if it were an official visit or a visit by invitation.

And when she had previously asked the king, "How can I come to the palace without an appointment?"

The king answered her, "My time is always free for you, Zabiba, my beloved."

Then she said, "You should not spoil me like that. For a common woman does not know the limitations of her attraction."

And the king answered her with a smile, "Didn't I tell you, Zabiba, that the kings need those people more who tell them the truth, rather than those who say, 'As you wish, my lord. As you wish, my great king!'?

"Friendly feeling and the joy of friendship! Isn't that what a king needs? To free oneself from the decayed notions which he received from the previous kings, that is the step needed to understand the life of the people in full. If I start limiting the one who is closest to me by a previously determined schedule, our times together will become a routine meeting. Once that begins neither you nor I would be able to change it, and we would act as we would if we were conducting official business. If we act more out of simple human desire, out of the feeling that directs two lovers, then even the serious work for the sake of the well-being of the people will be more productive."

"But be warned, my king. Forgive me, I do not mean warned in the normal sense."

The king laughed and said, "You see, you already began to weigh words, as if you were not a daughter of the people but a princess from a king's court."

Zabiba laughed and asked, "Do kings and princesses really weigh everything to such detail?"

"Not always. Not in the most important moments, but only in what they have accepted as the proper style of conversation at the court. Doesn't the one whose soul is empty care about excessive formalities? Didn't you tell me that yourself?"

"Yes, that is right, my king. A man whose essence is full of real things and whose day is occupied with real deeds won't observe formalities. He does not have time to waste on formalities, which accomplish nothing useful and aren't even an evidence of a proper upbringing."

While Zabiba was making her way from the external gates to the king's private chamber, and the king was preparing to meet her, he was tortured by uncertainty, and different thoughts swirled in his mind as he remembered different moments in their relationship.

Zabiba opened the door after knocking first, and the king shouted, "Come in!"

Then he fell silent from an unexpected sight. The face and hands of Zabiba were scratched all over. The king stepped towards her, but before he could embrace her, she threw herself into his arms, bursting into tears.

The king held her and stroked her head in silence. His fingers wandered in her hair until Zabiba had cried out all the tears that were welling up in her chest. That was their first meeting after the terrible sorrow that had befallen her. Two disasters, each being a source of great pain. She could not decide which one was bringing her more torment, that she was raped or that the one who raped her was her husband, the man who, among other responsibilities, had the duty to keep and protect her.

Sometimes she thought that the rape itself and the torments that it was causing weighed on her less than the torture in her soul because of the betrayal of her husband and the treachery of the criminal gang behind him which betrayed the king. The rape, perhaps, would have been less terrible if she had not found out that she was raped by her own husband. She tried telling herself that the rape happened independently of who committed it, and that her husband was only fulfilling the role of the stranger. If she had not happened to find out who it was, his name would have remained unknown and she would not have had to bear the pain of what was done.

Violence always brings a horrendous amount of pain, independently of whether it is a man who rapes a woman, an army of enemies invading the nation, or a law being violated by those who spurn it. But it is even worse when one is betrayed to the point of humiliation, whether by a country or a human being. Zabiba tried to ease the bitterness over the rape and the pain that was tormenting her soul. She said to herself, "But I resisted until I grew weak because of the blows and until my strength left me, and then I became like a breathless corpse."

Then she continued, "Yes, like a breathless corpse. Can a dead body be marred by the shame of rape? Can the shame of rape fall on the history of a country and its people when people are dying and there is no one in that nation with the strength hold a weapon in his hands?"

And she answered herself, "Yes, so it is; that ruler who allows "rape" while he is still alive and his people are not destroyed by the rape, that ruler is marred by shame. His people, if they continue to submit to such a king, will be covered with shame as well. Yes, rape is unbearable for any soul, for the history of a nation, or for any free man. A betrayal of a king is bitter, but a betrayal against the people and the nation and its history is a hundredfold more bitter."

Zabiba wiped her tears, but when she started answering the king's questions, telling him about what had happened, tears continued to flow making it difficult for her to speak. So she told her story, mingled with tears, until she had revealed everything to the end.

At first, the king was furious with rage, but then he composed himself. He listened with great sorrow.

He kept repeating out loud, "The plot of those who dared to do this was very painful and hurt me more than an arrow shot in my eye. But I swear by the Lord of Zabiba and by her purity my soul sees, my mind understands, and my conscience feels that we will wage a war against them, and we will not stop until we are directed by the will of Zabiba's God, Allah, merciful and compassionate. The king will wage war so that the heroes become heroes, so that the banner of truth flies high over the land, and so that the people have somebody who will be worthy of becoming its conscience and who will defend it. And if Allah, the host of the highest kingdom, desires for my soul to go up to him, that would be a great honor for me and then the sky would be a paradise and the earth would be its gates. May all the evil plotters be vanquished!"

The king immediately ordered his soldiers to bring Zabiba's husband to him because he was the key which could help unravel this conspiracy and lead them to the others who took part in violating Zabiba and in the attempts to kill the king. Zabiba said to the king, hearing that he was ordering her husband's arrest, "I beg you, my king, think of what the traitors would do if they find out that this bastard is arrested."

"And what more can they do, Zabiba?"

"The very thing that all despairing villains do when they are threatened by arrest and death, my king. They will take a risk and will attack you as is customary with the kings of Elam, and they will come into your palace."

"You are right, Zabiba. I will raise up my army and my spies, so that they are ready for the battle until the conspirators and traitors are dead or until they grow weak and the wind scatters them."

Zabiba said, "Yes, my great king, exactly so. And if you allow me, I will suggest to you one more thought."

"Of course, Zabiba. Speak, what do you want to say?"

"I ask for your permission to leave the palace. I will raise up the people so that they will help the army and then the villains will be desperate because they will be left with no place to hide, and we will have such a powerful moral and active support."

"Yes, Zabiba. Do so as quickly as you can. But I want a detachment of my loyal soldiers under the command of my faithful guard Abdullah to accompany you."

"Thank you, my king."

Zabiba said these words with pain in her heart, remembering what she had lived through because she had rejected an accompaniment of soldiers on her way from the king's palace home. That is why her rape had occurred. And still she would prefer to go to the people as one of them. The people does not like when persons of power come to it with great forces. The people thinks, and quite correctly, that the warmth of the people does not get through to the one who has on too many clothes. Multiple guards, which state officials use for appearance and threat, only distance themselves from the people. Only freedom and discipline can be a real basis for love. Officials should not surround themselves with more guards than is absolutely necessary. If the common people see that an official surrounds himself with guards without any valid reason, they are scared away from him. How can one who puts himself in unnecessary chains take chains off of others? The people, in spite of the king's acceptance and my special position by him, knew me as a common woman. If the people see a large detachment of soldiers led by the king's guard, they will mistake me for a princess or worse, a queen. And since they do not know the king as well as I know him, they will run away from me too. But what can I do? Come out without guards and by that endanger our plan of resistance against the conspirators? No. I have to agree to have some guards and entrust myself to the will of Allah. So thought Zabiba to herself after she asked the king's permission to go to the people.

When the king noticed that she was talking to herself, he asked her, "What is it, Zabiba? Do you have a different opinion about this?"

Zabiba came out of her deep thought and said, "No, my king, some thoughts came to mind, but I decided that your decision is best. I will go to the people, if you let me, and I will with all sincerity lift up prayers to Allah, that he might cleanse my face in your eyes. I believe with all my soul that Allah exists and that he is just. He is great and can cause the people to follow your lead in accordance with the high ideals and thoughts which I was telling you about and in accordance with what I know to be true."

"In Allah's name!" said the king.

Then Zabiba came closer to the king and kissed him on the forehead. The king embraced her. Then she knelt and bowed her head as a sign of submission, gratefulness, and love, as she did once when she came to his palace for the first time, and as she did from time to time when the king would entrust some important business to her, but not in their everyday relationship, for the king did not want simple formalities to kill and weaken the joy of their relationship.

When Zabiba returned to the palace, people were following her. They were shouting, "For our native land, for the nation, for faith, for faithfulness, for courage, for freedom, for justice, for truth!"

The roar of voices was getting louder, "Against treason, treachery, oppression, and persecutions!"

People crowded in the territory of the palace behind the outer wall, and Zabiba was carrying the banner while her heart was pounding in her chest. She was sitting on her white horse, with a sword on her belt. And the army united, and all stood before the king as their commander.

The conspirators found out that their plot was about to be exposed because of Zabiba's husband. This happened mostly because Zabiba's husband, though he did not show that he guessed that Zabiba knew everything, had in reality perceived that she did and had decided to run to the members of the conspiracy: emirs and those who supported them in the neighboring kingdoms. The conspirators decided to attack the king that very day, but they did not take into consideration that, thanks be to Zabiba and thanks be to Allah, the people would become the heart and the foundation of the king and that it would unite to give the army significant force. That is why when the traitors attacked the king's palace from all sides, a great power answered them back and they were taken by surprise with a rain of arrows. And every time they breached the external walls of the palace, the masses of people would not let them go far inside or disturb the order of the defense forces of the palace. The attackers would turn back when the spears, swords, and arrows of the soldiers and common people reached them, and even sticks had their place in this persistent and victorious resistance. Finally, the invaders were destroyed and the remainder fled, forsaking the bodies of the dead and wounded. They became shameful deserters after they had lost the highest human ideals and the good Lord's mercy. But at the very end of the battle, Zabiba was struck by an arrow, which pierced the leather shell which she preferred to iron chain mail.* The leather shell was what the common people wear when going to battle with the enemy, and Zabiba wanted to look different from the regular army and blend in with the people in both her appearance and spirit.

They took Zabiba to the king's chamber in the palace and put her on the bed, while one of the guards informed the king about her injury.

Even though the news struck the king a hard blow, and he was ready to go to Zabiba immediately, he controlled himself, saying, "I am afraid that the warriors will decide that I am leaving the battlefield after Zabiba was wounded and will stop the defense. Also, I am afraid that those who take notice will spread rumors about me. They will say that I was frightened by the fighting and left it under the excuse that I needed to check on Zabiba. Whatever may be, isn't it the law of the battle, that

---

* **EDITOR'S NOTE:** Chain mail - chest armor made of metal links tightly woven together.

the commander has no right to leave the battlefield in the most decisive moment? That is why I will avenge Zabiba by cutting off the heads of every traitor, and I will fight to the sure victory with the help of the God of Zabiba."

And he started charging onto the battlefield, thundering with his voice and crushing with his sword and spear. And when a sword or a spear would break in his hand, he exchanged it for another, until at last, the enemy was defeated.

As the grinders of the battle were rotating in such a manner, Zabiba lay on the royal bed and dictated to a secretary this letter to the king: "My dear beloved Arab: I do not want to call you 'my great king' so that the spirit of my word does not become burdened by titles and formalities. That is why I am calling you as it pleases my soul at this minute as I am saying farewell to you for the last time, having not even seen you. I called you by your name, may Allah protect it, as a symbol of love and respect for your people and your army.

"Out of my love for you, I do not reject your proposal for me to become your wife. This marriage was, and even now remains, my dream, speaking of the greatness of your soul and of the power of your love for me. I am answering you with the same inclination to self-sacrifice and generosity, though my words may appear to be strange. But when we speak of love and faithfulness, strange things often happen.

"I did not want you to make a decision about our wedding under the influence of these, but I wanted you to make this decision after the victory which you will soon win, if Allah desires so. As for me, I probably won't be in your world by then, but still I will be able to rejoice in this victory and will see it in all its glorious details. Don't the heroes who fall in battle live and prosper with the Lord?

Don't those who live there see everything that happens on earth? Yes, I will see your victory, our victory. I have yet to celebrate it. I want you to enjoy this victory and your new connection with the people. In order for this connection to occur I ask you to give the people the right to use any titles and names that will fit you. It will be necessary because the people who earned that right will be sincere in its decisions and will protect those convictions. They and you together will carry full responsibility for these decisions. In any case, I think that after the titles of kings and emirs were marred by such shame, the title of the king will no longer fit you. You need to be the leader of the people and the army, their guide to virtue, reconstruction, and victory. Get close to the people by using a title which would seem pleasant to them and through such actions which will distinguish you from the people, but not distance the people from you. Be one with the whole. Then the people and its army under your leadership can do the deeds which will bring glory to our country and the one who rules it, and they will become the builders of the glorious history of our great nation. Great is Allah.

"I ask you, do not forget me. I am dying by the hand of a traitor.

"Zabiba, the daughter of the people, the beloved of Arab.

"I am dying, long live the people!

"I am dying, long live Arab!"

***

Zabiba died and the king lived but a while until Allah took him, too. Every day, there were fewer and fewer kings. In all the palaces where they still reigned, evil and treason were still brewing. And the people, as before, would express its will whenever it had an opportunity to do so. The people are steadfast as eternity, as the Most Powerful desires them to be.

Zabiba died, and her eyes closed in the moment when her soul reached its place in the garden of eternity. The king was mourning her in great grief, saying, "Zabiba has died, but lives still among those who went up. She also lives among us as a great symbol. Her spirit remains to give inspiration to me and to the people with her faithfulness and wisdom, with her great soul and perseverance that was so pleasing to the people and to our native land. May it be so if such is the will of Allah, may he be pleased.

"Her soul remains with us and it soars above our heads with the souls of the heroes and of the righteous. The evil and villains have disappeared for a time. The people won the victory and the country is triumphant. The nation won by the mercy of the All Powerful. The invaders failed and were destroyed. The people had victory.

"I will meet you again, Zabiba, where your soul now dwells. Do you know how, Zabiba? Of course you do. You know that the road to you is my love for the people. I must provide opportunities for them and for their abilities in many different areas, and I must not place any unnecessary burdens upon them. The people must only carry the main responsibilities and their unshakable moral ideals. With the growth of the people's abilities and with the development of their understanding, the ladder by which I will climb to you will grow higher and higher.

"Go, and I will come up to you on the wings of my faith, if so be the will of my Lord and your Lord, Zabiba. You have achieved the highest level of freedom, Zabiba, of which you were telling me. That freedom is undoubtedly higher and deeper than the freedom which we know here on earth. But even that freedom is limited and not absolute. And do you know why, Zabiba? It is because with your heroic death you have gained such a position, which is acquired only in the struggle for the faith, and you could never take a level below the one you have deserved or even experience the lower level, and therefore you will be like the kings on earth, having such a distinction that you will stand apart from all others. You will be among the best. So it is with the kings, whom you criticize, and whom I now criticize with you. They cannot leave their palaces and live a normal life among the people, not on a regular basis, not even for a period of time, for the difference that is between them is like the difference between heaven and hell.

"Do you know that you cannot choose for yourself anything that is beyond the line which you drew with your heroic death for this nation and for this people? That is because absolute freedom is available only to the one who sits on the highest throne, your God and my God, Allah, merciful and compassionate. Only he alone, glory to him, can do everything that is higher, yet have the power to lower his abilities. Only he alone can hold any position or its opposite, without any element of duplicity. Heaven and hell, angels and demons, earth and sky, day and night, sun and darkness, are all by his command and from his wisdom. Now you see that there is no absolute freedom, even though we understand a concept of it, while there are still things that are higher or lower than our abilities. Allah granted us the highest understanding of our abilities and freedom.

"May Zabiba be in the heavens!

"And may she live on earth!"

***

People were sending Zabiba off and the sons of the people were carrying her coffin on their shoulders. Everyone tried to get her blessing. The people and the army were mourning her death and for a long time, the king was walking ahead of the procession right behind her coffin. They mourned her bitterly, and when the ground became her final dwelling place, the king ordered them to dig up the body of her husband, who was found amongst the mass graves of the slain in a hole far away from her grave.

When the people found out where it was, they stoned it and hurled at it everything their hands stumbled upon, including garbage. And it became a tradition in the life of the people to gather every year on that day, January 17* by the Christian calendar, in order to stone this base criminal, and with him all invaders and traitors. After cursing the infidels, people would go to Zabiba's grave with wreaths made of laurel and roses, where they lifted up their prayers for her, the heroine of the people, faithful to it in her life and in her death.

Then Arab announced that before going into the battle, Zabiba had become his wife, and that she had divorced her husband, the traitor. The king announced that he himself was the witness and he was the kadi** for he had the right to settle people's affairs.

This is the difference between the heroes who had fallen in the battle and those who lived, between the living and the dead. Between the fighters and those who betrayed Allah and their native land,

---

* **EDITOR'S NOTE:** January 17 - the date in 1991 on which the U.S. launched the first missiles against Iraq and the "Mother of all Battles," as Saddam Hussein titled it, began.
** **EDITOR'S NOTE:** Kadi – a judge.

the people and the nation. Between those who bring freedom to their people, nation, and country and those who forsake all that is dear and commit treachery.

Praise to the glorious life and to the death pleasing to Allah and infuriating to the enemies!

Great is Allah.

May all the evildoers be vanquished!

*** 

"Zabiba died, and may she also live!" So shouted the people in every corner of the kingdom, as if in contrast to "The king died, long live the king!" which was said when one of the kings died and another took his place on the throne, receiving his title by inheritance. These shouts were obviously directed against the order in which the king ruled the country, no matter how good he was.

So the battle that the people and the army waged against the conspiracy ended victoriously. The plot had not been intended to destroy the royal throne and the life of the king but to split the kingdom and to divide the spoil between the foreign kingdoms which supported the conspiring emirs and supplied them with weapons of destruction and annihilation. Though the soldiers of the army and the people who took part in the battle were driven by the highest ideals, there were others in the crowd who did not have the same values. They joined the king's forces in order to take advantage of the opportunity and to gain something for themselves. These were prosperous merchants and landowners, who had received all they owned by inheritance and not in reward for service and self-sacrifice in this fateful battle. There were also many other people besides merchants and landowners who pursued their own interests and were not led by the highest ideals and courage.

Doesn't it happen that way most of the time, if the nation does not care, or if the one who represents its conscience does not consider justice significant? Doesn't it happen that the army and the people die in battle, while somebody else who is neither pure, nor beautiful in the work of sacrifice, nor patient and heroic claims for himself all the glory and seizes what does not belong to him by right?

\*\*\*

And so the people's council came together with all its representatives. The other part, the ones that had wormed their way into the people, and who were in the minority should not have been there, because the battle had clearly shown who had the right to be a people's representative and who did not. But there were some weak personalities who came to the council who did not have the experience of the people and its capacity for sacrifice because the notions of loyalty to the people had not yet ripened in them, and they had not yet chased the weakness out of themselves. Their weakness was not only the weakness of fear, but many other weaknesses, including the one which praises those who deserve no praise.

That is why those who were in the minority gained entrance through the weak souls which allowed them to infiltrate and take places in the people's council which were not intended for them.

The people's council was made up of people from all classes of society, and each member had his own worth. There were men and women, military and civilians, peasants and craftsmen, and many others, but the greatest attention was drawn to a dignified woman, obviously a peasant by her behavior and dress. When she came into the hall, she was carrying a child, no older than one year. When she took her seat, she put the baby on her lap.

They started discussing the fate of royal power. The oldest among the gathered was conducting the discussion. That revered man was of outstanding character, which was obvious from his self-confidence. He had great physical strength which belied his age, which was getting close to sixty-five. Is not self-confidence the power of the one who uses it worthily?

The elder who headed the council pounded his fist onto the table at which he was presiding. To his right sat one of the generals, and to his left, a woman with a sword. By the appearance of the woman, it was clear that she had taken part in the massive resistance against the invaders of the palace.

Some of those present in the hall were deep in thought and some were talking to their neighbors, but when they heard the chief of the council pound on the table all grew silent. Then he asked for their attention with a solemn voice, the seriousness of which nobody would doubt, "Listen everybody! Before we begin, it is proper for us, and duty and gratitude demand the same, that we remember the souls of the slain heroes and first of all the soul of Zabiba, the daughter of the people, the symbol of the self-sacrifice and heroism of our great people and its courageous army. Let us honor them by rising to remember all the wounded and to pray for their healing."

The crowd that gathered in the hall did not allow the speaker to say anything else. After hearing the name of Zabiba, the hall exploded into applause. The shouts of joy and greetings mixed with sorrowful cries, and the tears flowed even from the eyes of those who never allowed themselves to shed tears. Even the military wept, though by their occupation and character they have to be as hard as flint, because in the battle they see their friends fall, yet still must continue doing their duty of war. So it is done in order for the fighting power of the army to remain strong and so that none of the fighters gets distracted from his duties and the common goal.

Even the military men wept when they heard the name of Zabiba. Does anyone deserve that eyes shed tears in his honor, and that hearts bleed except for Zabiba?

The roar of voices grew louder.

"Blessed be Zabiba, the daughter of the people and its inspiration!

"Blessed be Zabiba, the symbol of heroism and glory!

"May all the evildoers be vanquished!"

And nobody praised the king, except for one merchant who was present at the council without any right to be there. But those who sat by him made him stop, letting him know that what he said was creating dissonance. Besides, for one voice to be heard, it must possess absolute truthfulness in addition to great strength.

After everything that was said in the praise of the terrible and glorious battle, its symbols, and heroes, the audience calmed down. But those who were sitting by the woman who had a child on her lap were astounded that she was the only one of those present who did not cry. She kept silent and did not say a word. And when those who were sitting near her asked her about it or looked into her eyes, she smiled and said to them, "There are no longer any tears left in my eyes to weep. I had five sons and here on my lap is the son of the eldest of them. My tears will not make my sons come back.

They are among the symbols of the glory and heroism of our great people. And I came to support
those who need support, so that the babblers and
those who claim to be experts don't dilute the notions of heroism, courage, and gratitude, so that we
do not forget Zabiba and what our sons have done,
sacrificing their lives. Remembering what the great
people, in whose battalions my five sons were and
which were led by Zabiba by right, have accomplished, we must carefully preserve the security of
our land and our unity. We must choose the one
who, because of his extraordinary character, will
lead us, who will govern us justly now and in the
future. Only in that case will we foil the schemes of
our enemies; only then the self-sacrifice of the people will not be forgotten in the past, but will be
honored and will inspire the sons of the people to
sacrifice themselves if such is required of them.

"My sister (or my daughter)," she would say,
addressing the women who asked her, depending
on their age, "I concentrate all of my mind and
gather up all the strength that I have left in order to
remember forever the goal for which the blood of my
sons and Zabiba was shed. I am not weeping and
wailing with you so that I do not waste my last
strength, which I need to use for distinguishing
those who with their speech will try to lead us away
from the goal for which my sons, our sons, our heroes sacrificed their lives. I need to discern who
wants to betray the blood of Zabiba, the daughter of
the people and the soul of the people. That is why I
only listen and try to understand what is happening
around me, and do not preoccupy myself with anything else."

Hearing these words, the women stopped
wailing and the men wiped their tears with their
kaffiyas or with their hands and they all said to
that glorious woman, "Allah is with you and he will

strengthen you! We will all become the guardians who protect the principles for which the heroes of Iraq and his glorious daughters gave their lives, for which those who are still alive and those who now are in the presence of our Lord in heaven have been fighting. We will not allow impostors, charlatans or the worthless to take the self-sacrifice of our sons, brothers and sisters, our symbols and cover it with oblivion. We will not let them do that, and these things that we need to preserve from the lessons of our history, our native land, and our faithful people will be remembered for centuries."

\*\*\*

At that moment, everybody heard the chairman pound the table with his fist once again, and they stopped talking. After they had all released a portion of the tears that had accumulated, tormenting their chests, their souls were more obedient and they stopped disturbing the order which was required to keep calm and discipline in the hall.

The chairman of the council, whose name was Abd Rabbigi* said, "I want to remind you of the order of speaking in this hall. First of all, you need to speak of the main goals of this council, and not try to impress us with your words, because gold remains gold even if there is dirt on it. But if gold is polluted with dross then you certainly will have to polish it until all the corrosion is off, before people start believing that it is gold.

"Everyone to whom the majority of the present company allows the privilege will speak on the topics determined for the day, but nobody can speak twice on the same question if there are still

---

* **EDITOR'S NOTE:** Abd Rabbigi—literally from Arabic means "The slave of his lord."

others that have not had a chance to speak. Everyone who wants to speak must ask for permission by raising his right hand. The right to speak will be granted by the chairman. If you have no objections or corrections to the order of the meeting, let us go to the topics of discussion."

Nuri Chalabi* raised his hand. The chairman allowed him to speak and it was obvious to everyone that Nuri was from the number of those who belonged to the nobles of this world. He had no clear position in relation to the people or the army, and he had entered this council undeservingly.

He stood up and said, "We used to allow the right of speech to the best people in society first, and not to everybody without distinction. Why are you breaking this tradition?"

The chairman said, "Our council is a law unto itself. We reach decisions by the opinion of the majority and the people that get to make those decisions submit to the council and its decisions in their lives."

One of the military men raised his hand and said, "I agree with the chairman, but I wanted to add something. If we are ready to accept all the old ways as they are, then why would we have even gathered here?"

The majority presiding in the hall clapped.

Ahmad Al-Hasan asked to speak by raising his hand. It was obvious from his appearance that he was one of the outstanding people who had led the resistance against the invaders. He was about forty years old. When the chairman gave him the right to speak, he rose and said, "It is hard to conduct the meeting this way and we might have done well by listening to our friend here (he pointed to-

---

* **EDITOR'S NOTE:** Nuri Chalabi – An obvious reference to Ahmad Chalabi, an outspoken leader of a London based opposition movement against Saddam Hussein and his government.

ward Nuri Chalabi) who suggested that we change the order of the speakers. But, may I ask, how does he have the right to think of himself as one of the better people of the society, and therefore the right to speak before others? On what grounds did he come to that conclusion?"

When Nuri Chalabi answered that he had inherited that right from his predecessors, Ahmad Al-Hassan continued, "That which has been passed down to us in the traditions is observed by those who respect traditions and by those who had been forced to abide by them as a duty, without their consent, by people who have the power to do so. Now our friend Nuri Chalabi has no power here. Here, inheritance is divided by the right that one must first earn. We do not believe the things that you say, and we are not the sons of your father for you to give us your inheritance. You cannot impose your order on us, which would be convenient to you in the system of power based on the inheritance of the throne. We are gathered here for the very purpose of discussing that order, and there are enough people here who want to change it."

When he saw that his reasoning had no grounds, Nuri Chalabi protested, "Do you mean to say that you will change the order of the royal succession?"

Even though he was trying to show surprise, his words sounded shaky and uncertain. While Ahmad Al-Hassan smiled and said, "Yes, if two-thirds of those present here decide so, we will change the regime."

Nuri Chalabi said, "Will you change the king too?"

Ahmad Al-Hassan answered in the name of the people, "Yes, we will change the king. We will change the one who became a king with no consultation of the people, due to the power and politics of the foreign empires which appoint kings in these lands, including the king of our own great country, against the wish and will of the people.

"Now the will of the people has declared itself, and the unjust will and foreign powers cannot force their influence on us. Those who represent the people and its military forces have the right to express their decisive opinion of what the people need and what is not acceptable for it."

Nuri Chalabi, who had come to the meeting deceitfully and did not deserve to be there, grew silent and could find nothing to say in reply.

Then the chairman of the meeting said, "I would ask you not to discuss a question which is not yet on our agenda. Let us continue our meeting."

He repeated, "Is there anybody in the hall who has any objections to this order of conducting the meeting?"

***

The mother of the five heroes who had fallen in the battle raised her hand. The chairman let her speak, and she said, "Every meeting should have a purpose and goals determined at least as a starting point. If we have not decided under which banner we will conduct this meeting, I think that nobody would object to the fact that we gathered here to give glory to our heroes."

The audience filled with shouts and applause.

The mother of the heroes continued, saying, "Truly, Zabiba, the heroine of the people and its inspiration is a symbol of its heroism and self-sacrifice. That is why I suggest that we bring in her portrait and place it high over the table of the chairman of the meeting, so that to all of us it will feel that she is over our heads and so that she could be seen by everyone sitting in this hall. This way at least, the main direction of our council will be defined."

The chairman said, "The suggestion of the mother of the heroes to place the portrait of Zabiba over our heads in the center of the hall of the council deserves respect."

He pounded the table and said, "Now that it is clear that the majority agrees with the order of conduct for this meeting, let us discuss the questions on the agenda for the day.

"The main question that must be handled today is the question of power, about which Zabiba reminded the king in her advice. She said that the king must make the will of the people the determining factor in the form of the government and the order of the execution of power. And since the people have received their freedom, they need to declare their will."

Even though the king himself was not present and the will of the people had gained great significance in the establishment of its representatives, many did not want to discuss that question. The reason for that hesitation was probably their trembling before the government or their fear before the person of the ruler or their respect of the position which the king now occupied, and also Zabiba's attitude toward him, which could be easily perceived from her letter. And that attitude did not end until one of the people's representatives, whose clothes were still covered with the blood of the battle in which the blood from his wounds had mingled with the blood of those whom he slew with his sword and his kinjel, said, "None of us here has any evil thoughts toward the king, especially after he fought with us, but he would not be able to remain a king without the support of the people and the army. He could not resist those who contest with him over the royal throne, the emirs, on the basis of the saying: "If there is no good choice, choose the least of all evils. His father and his other predecessors made us suffer and the people did not know anything from them except misery and hardship. If I were to show you my back, you would see it as those of thousands whose backs were burned by whips of executioners, leaving permanent marks on them. Enough of the hunger, backwardness, and humility which fell upon us because of our rulers. Even when we say that this king is different from all other kings, we are the ones responsible for the fact that he is considered better than others in his character. Isn't it Zabiba, the daughter of the people, fulfilling the will of the people, who was responsible for making him take a different position and made him into a different man? Isn't it the people who did good to the king, including putting faith in Allah in his heart, though he was an infidel before? Isn't it the people who saved his life and his manly dignity, not even mentioning his royal honor before the face of the invaders and their conspiracy? And we did all that in order to put a king over our heads yet again? Even if we can vouch for the personality of this king and for the fact that the people accept him and that the country accepts him and that in general we will trust him, who will vouch for those who will inherit his throne after him? We don't want a youth, or worse, a child reigning over us, do we? We do not want our children and ourselves to be under the rule of some madman from among the children or grandchildren of this king, do we?"

The audience drowned in laughter, and then to show their agreement with what the speaker said, they applauded.

He continued his speech, "Whatever may be, I ask you to make a distinction between the personal opinion of each of us about our king and our general constructive opinion about the regime of royal power, so that we don't confuse things."

***

Another man raised his hand; from his appearance, it was obvious that he was one of the merchants who conduct trade between Iraq and the kingdom of Elam. He said, "Royal power is a reality, whether we accept it or not. This has been our regime from the ancient times and the people are already accustomed to it. How will we continue trade with other kingdoms if there is no stability in our land or in our country?"

One of the people sitting near him nodded, and the merchant thought to continue, but was interrupted by the chairman, "Do you want us to simply live with what we have not chosen and settle for what we have inherited just because that would serve your interests?"

The merchant continued, "We must resign ourselves to the existing situation, so that trade can flourish, because the familiar path with all of its imperfections is better than a road that leads to who knows where, even if the second road seems better at first. The wisdom of the people teaches us well, 'If you cannot cut the hand off, you had better kiss it!'"

One of the people, having asked permission to speak, asked a question, "And who is better, you with all your possessions or your father, the carrier, who at one time hauled goods for the merchants at the market? Why didn't you inherit the position of your father? Do the people have to multiply your riches and accept injustice, just so that somebody could get rich, like you got rich at the expense of the merchant who hired you as a clerk out of respect for your father? When the merchant died, he had nobody left but his only daughter. You pocketed all of his possessions and now you want everything to stay the way it is, as it pleases you, including the royal succession, so that you can keep your ill-gotten gain and so that you can maintain the patronage of those officials whom you bribed to buy their silence and protection? Is it fair, my friend, for us to continue making the same mistakes, protecting somebody else's dishonest interests, while the people bear and will continue bearing the burden of something that should have been radically changed a long time ago?"

Applause broke out in the audience, and the one who had raised the question stormed out of the hall, not looking at anybody as he went. He left the council and cursed the day when the people acquired a position which gave it firmness and victory over the invaders, the will and the desire to debate and the determination necessary for speaking the words of truth.

***

Shamil, about forty years old, raised his hand. When the chairman granted him permission to speak, he gave an extensive speech about gratitude and faithfulness, about respect for the law and tradition, all with a certain rehearsed theatrical flair which, however, could not fool a keen mind. He said, "I am not going to defend the royal regime, but I want to say that our king has a right to reign because he fought with us. Zabiba is our symbol, and she was pleased with him even to the moment of her very death."

So did he say: "fought with *us*." But before he could continue speaking, one of the men sitting near him, who was among the leaders of the resistance, appealed to the chairman, "Mr. Chairman, the speaker said that the king was fighting with *us*, implying that the speaker himself was among those who fought in our great national battle against the invaders and conspirators, but that is a lie. This man did not fight with us. He was speculating on the market, weakening our currency for his own profit. He was reselling food and making money at the expense of the people. I ask the chairman to demand an explanation from this man before the council. When and how did he fight with us, he or his father? I say this, because his father was speculating currency at the market as well. Both he and his father were on more than one occasion brought to the court, accused of counterfeiting. The current royal regime, with its multiple loopholes and decaying jurisdiction and law enforcement system, allowed them to escape punishment every time. Sometimes they bribed the officials and at other times, they produced forged documents *proving* their innocence."

Shamil the Jew stood and said, "I fought in that battle against the invaders. I paid a monetary price for the military service. I did not think that mobilization for the war against the foreign invaders was a task for me, but I did send a slave of mine to fight and paid him four times more than usual, plus I gave him some food and clothes that I did not need any more."

Then an officer, one of the generals and leaders of the resistance, rose up and said, "I wonder how you can listen to this charlatan? How could he be given the right to even speak at this council, the sacred nature of which is reflected in its purposes? I know Shamil and I know that he has a son who is past twenty years old, but he hid him from the battle. He never served in the regular army because he always found a way out, using all kinds of excuses.

I know for sure that Shamil's son was not among the fighters during the heroic resistance, when our country and our people were targeted by a cruel and treacherous conspiracy. When the general mobilization was announced, it was Shamil's duty to join the army, but he wasn't among the troops either. Besides, he was helping the sons from other wealthy families to escape abroad so that they did not have to join the army. By this, he struck a direct blow to our country and our people, because without the army, our country becomes helpless before those who desire to conquer it by force. For this treachery, Shamil must be denied his citizenship, and the one who is not a citizen has no right to represent the people at this council. I suggest that we expel him from this gathering and also from our nation."

Everybody enthusiastically supported the idea (except for a small number of those present who kept silent for fear that if they spoke, the representatives of the people would simply explode with rage), and shouted, "Away with Shamil, get him out of here! Throw him out of our council! Exile him from our land! May he be cursed from this day and till the end of his life!"

People were pushing on him and he jumped up and rushed from the hall, out of his wits with fear, falling on his way and scattering his belongings. He did not even stop to pick them up but scrambled to his feet and fled.

***

A military man wearing no armor asked to speak. By looking at his clothes, it was clear that he too, had not fought in the resistance. Everything about him revealed that he was one of the rear camp officers from the capitol, where those like him spend all of their time getting promoted, independently of what they truly deserve. That is very different from how it happens on the front lines or in the active forces. He rose to his feet, with the freshness of his face, hands, and neck reminding one of a housewife from a rich family. After introducing himself, listing the things he had accomplished so far (first of all, publishing several booklets and books on etiquette, the order of food consumption, and rules for interaction of the officers in the dining hall) and explaining that he was working on the question of supplies and military trade, he said, "Truly, our king inherited the throne from his father. To deprive him of that heritage would mean issuing a law which would deprive all sons of the people of what they inherited from their fathers and that is a very dangerous practice. I think that depriving the people, including the army, of the right to inherit anything material or immaterial from their fathers is something that neither the people nor the military would approve of. It is unlikely that I would misrepresent the truth if I were to say that all those here who have inherited anything from their fathers would not agree with that, except, perhaps, those who never knew their fathers or did not inherit anything from them, because they had nothing to pass on."

Another man asked to speak. He was among those who had fought in the battle. That was obvious from his appearance, clothes, and a bandage fixed on the wound on his left shoulder. He said the following, "I thank Allah and the leaders of the resistance, among whom is also the chairman of this council, for this opportunity to discuss everything in this meeting. I am thankful that they chased all weakness away from the souls of those who were weak, because of their faith and service to the noble cause of our people and our country. I ask you to allow me to point to the weaknesses of those whose weaknesses need to be pointed out, because these people have become so immoral that they are not capable of seeing their own weaknesses. They are so accustomed to them that they are not even ashamed of them any more, but on the contrary, they speak of these weaknesses as if that is the way all people should conduct themselves.

"There is much wisdom in the ancient proverb: 'A candle frightens the darkness as faith frightens a shaitan.' This wisdom strengthens our position. And this council is the true banner for those who started their journey in the right direction, and a rising of the sun which will scare the darkness away. I want to say, in short, my brothers and sisters, comrades and children; I address those who fit that description. The officer who was speaking before you just now found his way into the ranks of our glorious army through the negligence of those too weak to express their opinion. His father was an army general. He always sought the favor of the father of our king and always told him that the highest honor and prize for him was to hold the stirrup of the horse when the king was mounting the horse and to kiss his feet. So did he kiss the shoe of the previous king until Allah took him away. The mother of this officer invited men and women to frivolous mixed parties, and when the king would choose a woman he liked, the mother would go and find out if the woman would submit to the king's desire. While the party was going on, the mother would take the woman to the king's chambers. This officer and his wife did not care about anything. They simply attended those nocturnal parties. I could now order hundreds of officers to come here so that you could ask how many of them were invited to his house for a so-called dinner party. Ask them whether they know how the bedrooms are situated in his house. Have they ever been in the house in the absence of the host? Ask them if they happened to come to his house without their families. Whether the hostess ever invited them to have some refreshing drinks, tea, or coffee, while her husband was not at home. This officer never trained anybody, whether in the field or anywhere else. If you ordered him to prepare a detachment of soldiers for defense or attack, he would never be able to do that. I don't even have to mention that he never took part in any of the battles in which his army engaged, even though that is a part of his responsibilities. So how could he, my comrades and my children, my brothers and sisters, how could he sit here with us? Can this man carry the name of a warrior in our fearless army? Could this man be allowed to wear the uniform which became a symbol and honor of the one wearing it?"

Applause could be heard in the audience and in the sound of the voices of those who praised the army and the people, while the military men shouted, "We have nothing in common with you! It will be an insult to us if he remains in our ranks."

And again, applause and shouts followed, from which it was clear that those present were supporting the warriors. When the officer who took such a shameful position was leaving the hall, it seemed as if even the air were making it hard for him to walk. And if it weren't for the uniform he was wearing, blows would have covered him from all sides.

***

A man who was nicknamed "Hunter-of-emirs" raised his hand. Everybody knew him by this nickname instead of by his real name, which had been forgotten somehow after his heroic deeds during the battle. With his spear, arrows, and even kinjel, he killed emir and merchant left and right, as if he were an expert in doing that and were meant to hunt only them.

Even though he had no horse, he overcame his enemies anyway. He was like a wolf attacking a sheep that got behind the herd. Because of his incredible speed and strength, nobody could escape from him alive. He would catch up with the horse and grab it by the tail or by the stirrup because he wasn't very tall. In a moment, both the horseman and the horse ended up on the ground, and he on the chest of the horseman. He would immediately cut the emir's head off and plunge his spear into the emir's chest with such strength that it would go deep into the ground.

Because he was so short, he might have been called "shorty" if they weren't afraid to give him such a nickname after the heroic deeds that he had done. His glory spread everywhere, and the people knew how he had thrown down one emir after another, and how skillful he was in turning away from the point of a spear, a sword, or an arrow.

When the chairman motioned for him to speak, the Hunter-of-emirs mumbled something incomprehensible. His face reddened at first, then grew yellow because he was embarrassed by the position in which he found himself and which was suffocating him, as if preventing him from speaking. When he realized that he could not be loud and clear enough for those who gathered in the hall to hear him, he asked his neighbor to help him. He grabbed him by the arm, helping him get up from his seat and placed him beside himself. From the way he was acting, people understood that he was mute and was asking his neighbor to communicate with those who were sitting in the hall. His neighbor was his old friend and one of the bravest fighters in the national army of military resistance.

The Hunter-of-emirs at times mumbled something, at times sounded like a clucking bird, and at times used different signs while his friend would put his words into regular phrases for the people who listened to him, as if he were interpreting from one language into another. He said, "Greetings to you, my brothers and sisters, and praise for the sacrifices you have made. I bend my knee in the name of Allah, great and most powerful, before the most important, the most pure rivers, all the rivers of blood shed by the warriors who fell in the battle. I am a humble slave of Allah, the Hunter-of-emirs, as you called me, and it is because of Allah that I am so humble. Nobody knows my story and nobody knows why I was only slaughtering emirs and wealthy merchants.

"I did not shoot arrows, strike with my spear, or cut with my sword anyone other than them. I did not even strike those who wanted to take my life in the heat of the battle. Even if I saw that they wanted to kill me, I would find a way to dodge the blow without hitting them back. I did not waste my strength on those who were not emirs or wealthy merchants, who accumulated their riches dishonestly and unfairly because they are worms which gnaw on the trunks of every noble tree of our kingdom; they are the parasites of life and a deadly poison, dirt soiling the white clothes. So that you could understand all this, here is my story.

"I used to serve with one of the emirs and I had his trust. He taught me military art so that I could guard his back day and night, when I was accompanying him on the hunt or on outings for other business.

"During one of these trips, the emir tried to ask permission from one man to marry his daughter, a young girl of amazing beauty. Her father was a sheik, a man of the highest reputation and noble deeds and thoughts. When her father explained to the emir that his cousin wanted her and that she wanted that young man, the emir said that he would postpone the conversation for another day and threatened to kill the sheik if he would not allow the emir to marry his daughter. The father, fearing the consequences of disobedience, was forced to marry them. The emir decided to take her right there in his camp which was situated right near the Arab tribe of the girl's father, instead of bringing her to the capitol and having a wedding there as emirs usually do. To tell you the truth, he was showering her father with expensive gifts. But all the presents gave the father nothing but grief for his daughter and sorrow over her marriage to the emir, because by the traditions of this honorable man and his tribe it was customary to give away daughters only to their cousins and to nobody else. The girls would choose one of them. Some would agree to marry, others would disagree, while the fathers would seal their decision with their confirmation. That tradition was highly respected even by those people who did not practice it themselves, because that tradition kept all the social differences between the two sexes to a minimum and made family life stable and steady. Harmony between husbands and wives was growing and conflicts happened very rarely.

"The girl's father understood that her marriage to the emir, imposed by force, would be a disruption of a tradition which he could not break, but which he was supposed to guard and to insist that it be observed in his tribe. Isn't it a shame for the sheik if he allows some foreigner to break the traditions and customs of his tribe?

"On the first wedding night, or I should correct myself, in the noon of that day my lord, the emir (he pronounced the phrase 'my lord' with much sarcasm) tried to take the girl in his tent, but she rejected him and treated him rather rudely. When he responded to her likewise, she threatened him using harsh words. This is what she told him, 'You behave not like an emir, but like a worthless brute. Otherwise you would not have agreed to sleep with a woman who does not want you but on the contrary hates you because you force her to be intimate with you! Don't you know how much women hate those who force them to do a lawless act which they do not want?'

"Then the emir said that he had taken her with permission from her father. Then she answered angrily, "You did not ask any permission; you stole me from my father, from my family, and my tribe. We despise the very idea that our name will be linked with your name or with the names of those who are like you. I will always think of you that way and my opinion will never change.'

"When the emir heard such words from her, he had to leave the tent. I heard everything because I was waiting near the tent, ready to do anything that my master might command me, and she was pronouncing her words very loudly, so that everyone anywhere near the tent could hear her."

At the word "master," he smiled in disgust and so did the majority of those listening. He continued, "When the emir saw me while he was getting out of the tent, he tripped on his robe and his ukal fell on the ground. I picked up the ukal, and giving it to him, I blew off the dust, as if I were spitting in the hateful face of the emir. But I wanted to spit on him even more when, before he took the ukal from me and put it on his head, he said, 'Bring her a jar with a chamomile brew and tell her that your master loves her and that his eyes have had no sleep since the day he saw her by the lake. Ask her to have mercy on your master, or else he will lose his temper and kill her.'

"I asked him, much surprised, 'Will you really kill her, my lord? How will you do so if we are the guests of her tribe? Do you want to bring shame upon the tribe by killing her on her wedding night? What will people say?'

"He answered me, and it was clear that he was angry. 'If she does not submit to me and won't sleep with me this day, put poison in her food.'

"In order to test the measure of his evil plan, I asked, 'Do I have to give her the poison, my lord?'

"He said, 'Yes, you will put the poison in her food or drink and then we'll say that a snake bit her. We will find an adder, kill it and throw it on the floor of the tent and tell them that we killed it after it bit the girl, but we were too late to help her and save her life.'

"I asked, 'Are you serious, my lord?'

"He answered abruptly and decisively, 'Yes, I am absolutely serious. If this miserable bitch will not submit to me this night, and after that you won't give her poison, I will kill both you and her. So you have nothing else left but to go and convince her.'

"When I tried to calm the emir's rage, he said, 'Listen, everything will be the way I said. I know one proverb, 'If you see that a neighbor has a candle and you cannot steal it to light up your own house, break it with a shot of an arrow so that it goes out or otherwise it will burn up the house of its owner."

"When the hateful emir revealed to me what was on his mind, I realized that he had decided to do that evil.

"I said to him, 'I will try, but I pray you, do not hurry me, but give me the rest of today and the whole of tomorrow.'

"He answered me in a tone which allowed no contradiction, 'A part of the coming night and the rest of today. Not a minute longer.'

"Having asked permission from my lady, I came into the tent."

The audience noticed that both the mute and the one who interpreted his gestures and muttering both grinned at the words "my lady."

The mute continued his story. "I told her respectfully, 'My lady, I have heard everything that you said to this man, I mean the emir, and understood everything. I agree with you about everything that you think and with everything you said to the last detail, but I beg you to show mercy and listen to me. Allah is my witness that I want nothing else but for you to help me to save your life. To save your life, not mine, your life and the honor of your father, and not my life. Not my life.'

"When she heard me say 'not my life' twice, she looked at me in surprise, lifting her head which she had been holding down before, thinking that anybody who was in the camp of the emir was an enemy to her and to her father, an enemy to her fiancé and to her tribe, and, she would also add, an enemy of any free and noble person.

"I told her what the emir had told me and especially insisted that if she were not to show submission, whether by her own will or because of my persuasion, one could only guess what would happen to her. But I added to that, 'Even though I told you all this, I swear by Allah, that if you were to command me to kill the emir, I'd kill him in order to free all that is sacred, and if you were to order me to go with you to the house of your father, I would do what you told me. But of course you un-

172

derstand that this would bring shame on your head and on the head of your good father and on your noble tribe. I am only telling you this so that you understand that my purpose is not to save my self, but to save you and your honor. I am not pursuing my own interests, but I am willing to obey every motion of your hand.

"She looked at me with a long gaze, as if she were hypnotized, and in her gaze there was such a readiness to something, I could not even imagine what. I felt uncomfortable because of this gaze, because I could not suggest to her any other decision except to submit to something which was repellent to her soul, and I am a courageous man. Is it right for a man like me to persuade a woman to submit to a man whom her soul does not accept? If we could only cut the heads off of all the pimps, independently of whether they do their dirty deeds among the poor people or for the emirs and rich merchants!

"She said to me, 'Good for you, may Allah bless you. I will tell the emir that your arguments convinced me, so that you don't lose his favor and can stay by me so that I can seek your counsel. Keep secret what we just talked about and I promise not to tell him of the details of our conversation.'

"I was flying on the wings of joy because I had accomplished this unpleasant task."

The mute stopped, and tears streamed down his cheeks, flowing like an autumn rain onto the ground.

He wiped his tears and stood silently, and with him all who were sitting in the hall hushed, waiting to hear the words of his story, which the interpreter would transfer from his signs. The time was passing and the chairman had to ask, "So what happened next?"

"I passed on her words to the emir, that he could go into her tent. I heard how she told him, 'Your man convinced me with his arguments and I will submit to you, but I have one request. I beg you, do not disappoint me. My family and my tribe have a tradition. A woman that marries an outsider stays with him at his house as a guest for a month, so that the wedding may be considered complete. All that month, her husband hosts her father and her tribe.'

"She said to him, 'I do not think that you want me to be treated worse than other women in my tribe who married outside of the tribe. If you accept my condition, I will be in your debt, but if you don't, it will be your own fault that I will always have the feeling that you raped me.'

"When he tried to shorten the time, Zabia* did not agree.

"And even though he told her that every day of those thirty would cost him a herd of a hundred camels or a thousand sheep, or two pounds of gold, Zabia did not change her conditions.

"I found out about that later during our journey when we were crossing the desert on our way to the capitol, after the emir could not resist her request as he sought her favor. On the second week after we came to the capitol, the conspiracy broke out and the battle took place. And we decided, having talked it over, to join the resistance. I went as I am, and she dressed as a youth. At that day, I did not yet know what plan had ripened in her head. I did not know whether she was plotting something or just trying to win some time, waiting for the consolation from the Master of great joy, merciful and compassionate."

---

* *EDITOR'S NOTE:* Zabia - literally in Arabic means "antelope" or "gazelle."

And the mute started crying loudly, but in a little while he controlled his tears. In his eyes, rage and pride were burning.

He asked with strength and conviction, "You will probably ask where and how I lost my tongue?"

"On the next day after we came to the capitol, the emir showed up at my door with a dozen of his guards. They came suddenly, tied my hands behind my back, and tied my legs. They threw me on the floor, and one of them stepped on my jaw and said, 'Get your tongue out! We will tie it with a rope, so that you don't say the things that the emir entrusted to you.'

"I believed them, or at least I had to do what they told me, and they tied a rope to my tongue then pulled it hard and cut my tongue off with a kinjel. This crook (pointing his thumb over his shoulder) was holding the rope in his hand!"

Everybody shouted, "Great is Allah! Away with the emirs and kings!"

"Away with the royal power!"

"Blessed be the people!"

"Blessed be the army!"

The mute continued his story. "I saw among the guards that came with the emir three sons of rich merchants, whom he took with him to save them from military service and so that they would be with him in his parties and nocturnal adventures. Isn't it clear now why my purpose in this holy battle was to kill only emirs and rich merchants? Isn't it clear what the disadvantages of the kingship are? But now Allah has opened our eyes. Here is my witness. You can listen to him if you want to know more."

While his friend was interpreting his gestures, the Hunter-of-emirs went into the next room and came back with a man whose hands and legs were tied and whose mouth was plugged with a rag.

He took out the rag, untied his feet and asked, ges-
ticulating nervously, while the interpreter translated, "Are you an emir?"

"Yes."

"Tell them, I overcame you in a battle, standing face to face and not by mischief, as you are
used to, didn't I? I grabbed the horse on which you
were sitting by her neck and knocked her down.
Then I jumped on your chest and disarmed you. I
tied your hands and your legs and dragged you off
the battlefield and then put Zabia to guard you, until all was over. Is this how it was?"

The emir was silent. Embarrassed, he hid his
eyes while the mute made clucking sounds in fierce
rage, "You could hear everything I was telling to the
gathering, because your ears and your eyes were
open when I left you in that room. So tell them, do I
speak the truth or not? If you do not know the answer, I will find somebody else who will speak instead of you."

When he said that, someone stood up in the
audience. Everybody thought that it was a young
warrior of the resistance, because he was in the full
military armor, and his clothes commanded respect
and spoke of grandeur. But then he removed the
cover from his face and spoke in a woman's voice,
"It is I, Zabia, the daughter of the sheik of my tribe.
Truly every sound, every word that has been spoken by the Hunter-of-emirs is true. I swear to Allah
that he speaks the truth. But I beg you to give me
this man and not to torture him, because I swore to
Allah to forgive him if I overcame him. I said to this
creature when I asked for a month's delay that if he
gave me my wish, I would be in his debt. I don't
think that the Hunter-of-emirs would want me to be
indebted. How do I know and how would you know
if perhaps my misfortune was added to the misfortune of the Hunter-of-emirs and the grievances of

all who were made desperate by this emir, his courtiers, and the courtiers of the kings so that Allah would become angry with them and let us overcome? Doesn't Allah deserve that we fulfill our promises that we make before his face, even if no one but he knows about them? So that you understand, I will tell you that I swore to Allah to protect the life of this fool, and that is why I ask my brother, the Hunter-of-emirs, who overcame him in the battle, to give his permission not to kill him, but to throw him into prison until the end of his days. So I will give him my debt back and return the bride money which he paid for the wedding, if my father agrees to the wedding and if the Hunter-of-emirs would grant my request. And if my father does not bless my marriage, let him do with the bride money anything he wants."

The Hunter-of-emirs, wiping off his tears, said, "As you please, my lady and my sister, if only Allah does not wish differently. I tell you before this whole gathering of these good people, men and women, that you can do with him anything that you want. I am certain that after he gives you a divorce, you will let him go and will not even throw him into prison.

"I admit that Allah gave me the strength to overcome him in the battle, but I wanted to win over him not because of my hate for him for what he had done to me. I fought because of my rage directed against the rotten regime of power of which he is a wicked example, and for victory in the cause of the people.

"From this moment on, especially if my lady Zabia requests it, I do not at all care whether he will continue living like a cursed and dishonest wretch or if he will die a shameful death which nobody will regret."

Zabia interrupted him, "There is yet no marriage between me and this maggot and I've heard from my father that the bride's money has not been used yet. He accepted the bride's money from this maggot in fear for his tribe and not just for my life and his. And this man never took me, so I do not owe him anything."

The Hunter-of-emirs said, "Nonetheless, now he is your property and you can do with him whatever you want. His influence and importance among the people are equal to nothing; it is the same as if he had died. However, he died even before that, when his conscience and the sprouts of goodness, nobility, and faith died within his soul. I know people like him; I know that their influence ends when they lose the regime which support them. I want my sister and my lady to know all this, because she believed me. And this bastard who cut my tongue off probably thought that he would be able to cut the truth off, too. He did not realize that even without that truth being made known, his deeds, including the fact that he cut my tongue off and that he tried to force you to marry him, would be enough to condemn him.

"Deal with him as you wish. You can do whatever you want; you don't have to feel like you owe me anything. I am also free in my choice and I think that you have paid your debt to me."

Shouts and applause were heard in the audience, including curses and epithets toward the emir and the royal regime.

\*\*\*

Another man raised his hand, asking for permission to speak. From his appearance, it was clear that he was a landowner but not a sheik; that is, he did not belong to the family or tribe of the region of which some thought when they saw him. He was one of those landowners who do not live in the village but only use it. He would give the peasants land to live on while they worked for him.

He got up when the chairman gave him permission to speak, and everybody knew that he was a landowner who lived in the city and managed his property in the country through mediators.

He said, "I do not have any personal feelings toward the king, especially after he joined the rabble under Zabiba's influence and became one of them. I do not prefer rulers who reign on the basis of certain principles or moral values, but rather I judge everything by whether or not it fulfills my personal interests. I know that my opinion about values won't be liked by the majority of those who are gathered here, especially after the well-known people have mixed with the people who are not known, and those who are familiar to us with those whom we'd meet only when we used the whip their backs. The only thing I am concerned with, and this I say to all classes represented here, is my personal interests, the interests of my family, our hard-earned wealth which we gathered by the sweat of our brows, and I am also concerned about the fate of our portion in the village."

When he said "by the sweat of our brows," many started laughing, mocking him, and one of the men sitting close to him said so that everybody could hear, "That's for sure. And in this meeting there is even more sweat on your brow. Aren't you ashamed of saying things like that? The only reason you sweat is because of the weight of your belly, which you gained by the sweat on the brows of others, who suffer your injustice and tyranny. And here is the proof that you are speaking a lie: on your face there are no marks left by the rays of the sun; they never touched it. My face is another story; it has been burned by the sun. So much skin has peeled off my face that my black eyes are hard to find in it, if you don't know where to look for them."

The audience drowned him out with applause.

The landowner continued, "I said that many won't like my words, but I like them and many others here might like them too. I swear by my faith that those here who have land and use other people's labor on it, instead of working themselves or making their own sons work on it, understand me. But unlike them, I prefer to speak about it openly while they sit here quietly.

"Do you know why I speak and they are silent? Because I do not know how to read or write, and I do not seek power. But there are some here who hope to get a high position in the new government, may it be royal or otherwise. That is why they are trying to win love from those sitting in his hall, and they are watching carefully how pleasure or displeasure is reflected in the eyes of those listening to them. Don't those who want to rise to power use the people responsible for making decisions? Isn't that how they do it? But I do not want to chain myself to a title or load myself up with responsibilities. I simply use power for my own interests, for my personal benefit. Doesn't a free person have the right to protect his interests?

"My method of protecting my interests is the following: I use the influence of those in power through my position and with the help of money. I am an owner of a large estate and beautiful palaces; I am the master of many servants and slaves; I have a court and guards. Do you know how I use the present regime? There are people who accept my words and sometimes my demands because I spend part of my enormous property on those who can do me a service. I give money to the chief of law enforcement and he obeys me and uses his whip against any rebel in my fields, and not only in the fields. I give money to the tax collector and he lowers the tax on my land, and what I gave to him comes back to me with extra. In this way, I deal with everyone who has power. It is within my interests to give to them in order to receive even more. I invite them to join me at the table with wine and gambling and I listen to their conversations about import, export, internal and external markets, and then I play my game to multiply my riches. My power is in making more money, and the one who has no money has no power.

"What privileges would the new power give, if I were to become a part of that government? Would it give me more privileges than I have now? Would it give me more land? The government which listens to the wishes of the people and follows them in everything is not capable of giving me more than I have now.

"I have inherited everything that I have from my father. And do you know how? My father, may Allah be merciful to him, called the king and his courtiers, ministers, and many other prosperous officials to a feast, where he served thousands of the most rare dishes, from camel meat to poultry. He covered the road leading from the gates of the king's palace to the door of his house with silk. This feast cost him a hundred thousand shekels, and then, on top of that, a loan taken from a Jew after they agreed on the percentage of interest that the Jewish usurer would get. The heads of the royalty were intoxicated with wine and desire, awakened by the women whom my father had invited there for that purpose, and the Jew cried out after making a toast to the health of the king and his long reign,

'What reward does the host of this feast deserve, O my great king?'

"The king asked, 'What do you mean, Shamil?'

"Shamil answered, 'I am just asking, my great king, whether the king will reward the host and whether his gratitude will match what people say about royal generosity?'

"Having called his main guard to himself, the king said in the hearing of everyone in the palace, 'In gratitude for the hospitality of our host, I give him all the land that he can ride through on his horse from dawn to nightfall. All these lands will be his property and he can use the labor of the peasants who live on these lands, to the right and to the left of him, as far as the eye can reach. All that for him, and may he prosper."

"All these lands I received by inheritance from my father, may Allah be merciful to him. The Jew gave my father a maid as a sign of his gratitude for taking the loan from him. My father married the maid, and I became the fruit of that marriage and the favorite of my father among all of my brothers, sons from other women. My father gave me the largest portion of his possessions.

"That is why I am not greedy, and I am quite satisfied with the land that I have. But I want to find out only one thing. Do you think to limit the land ownership or to leave it as it is? Are you planning to create a special order of rent to make our life harder and to allow our peasants to rebel against us, or not? And most importantly, are you going to leave us the right to use our money any way we want, or will you meddle in our affairs? After I hear your reply, which I hope will be sincere, as were my words, I will decide who I am with and in what direction I will go. It may be that the royal regime will end up being the dearest of all to me."

***

One of the women who took part in the resistance raised her hand. The chairman allowed her to speak and she stood up, as had been customary from the beginning of this meeting, or at least since the speech of the Hunter-of-emirs who stood up and was standing until he finished telling his story to the people of the council. She greeted the chairman and thanked her Lord, the God of the people and the army and not the god of the kings, emirs and merchants, who live in prosperity and for whom all is connected to their interests. Then she said, "I am the daughter of a peasant. We work on the land which my father rented from the government at a very high price. Our land was just outside of the city walls near a summer palace of one of the emirs. One of the princesses, when she wanted to entertain herself, would come to our vineyard to watch how we work. By the quality of her questions, it was obvious that she was an intelligent girl and wanted to know what was going on outside of her palace, and it happened that the closest place to her palace was our land where we grew grapes, gathered the crops, and sold them. If we did not succeed in selling what we harvested, we would dry the grapes and eat bread with raisins all winter. I was still a little girl and of the age at which they would still call me a child, but I remember everything that I want to tell to this council very well; I will not err in my story. Two of my sisters and I would always rush to get her a mat as soon as we saw her coming toward our vineyard in the evening. And our father would always bring her the best clusters of grapes. She wore dibadg and silk and carried such an aroma that I never knew before that and never have known since. When she was leaving, we would be pacing after her like hound dogs to catch the aroma of her perfume, which would remain in the air for a while after her departure. One day, after she accepted the grapes from the hands of my father as she had many times before, my mother decided that the princess was staying after sunset on purpose, so that we could not milk the cow. Because they led the calf to the cow thinking that we had already milked it, we would be left without supper, because we were sharing the cow's milk between our family and the calf, or to be more precise, the cow would only give the milk that would exceed what was needed to feed the calf and did not let us milk her when her udder had only enough left for the calf. I think that the real reason for my mother's irritation was her jealousy toward the princess, and not the milk that we were losing. She was afraid that the princess would lure my father away from her, though that was far from possible. The next day after the princess left, I saw my mother take a sickle and press it to my father's throat saying, 'If this happens one more time, I will cut your throat. Leave it to me. It is my responsibility to welcome the female guests in our house and in the vineyard. I will wash the grapes and give them to her in a bowl or on a plate.'"

Then the woman said with a smile, "From that day on, my father would not dare to do what was not proper for him to do any more. As you can see, a woman is capable of resisting her lot in life and even of resisting her husband."

The audience burst out laughing, while she continued, "The visits of the princess continued and she always tried to prolong her stay in our house. And when she was going back to her palace, she would go around the vineyard, taking a different road which would lead her to the walls of the palace, and then she would enter the palace from a back gate. And when my mother and I would come with her to the gate, she would always ask us to wait and whispered about something with the old woman who was waiting for her. Later we found out everything from her. One time we told her that we didn't have any grapes to give to her because the king's slaves would not let us go to our vineyard at night. And because they did not let us, it happened that there were no grapes left after people started coming to the vineyard at night, and we could not find out who those people were and why the king's slaves did not let us go to our vineyard anymore.

"The princess said that this was the very reason why she would burden us with her frequent visits.

"When she saw surprise on our faces, she said, 'The reason is in the constant feasts of the emirs and princesses. When they and their guests are tired of sitting in their palaces and the wine goes to their heads, they run out of the palace and play hide and seek on beastly terms in the vineyard. The women hide from the men or pretend to do so, while the men turn around under the supervision of an old woman who makes sure that they don't peek until all the women have had enough time to hide. Then, at the old woman's signal, the men start looking for the women in the vineyard and if a woman wants the man passing, she moves so that he can find her. And if the one who is near her is unattractive to her, she clings to the ground like a partridge hiding from a hunter, who will not give herself away even if he steps on her.

"'As for me,' said the princess, 'I could not live with these customs and this behavior, and so to save myself from embarrassment and so as not to interfere with the guests, I would run away to you. That is why I was never in a hurry to go back to the palace until I was certain that everybody had left it and was busy with their games. Then I would go to my room and lock the door behind me.'

"The princess continued her story, 'That is not the only reason why I distracted you from your many labors which, I realized from my conversations with you, are more than enough. The reason is also in the fact that among those wild cats who were chasing their prey, there was one emir whose face I'd rather never see, and I tried never even to speak to him.'

"I have to admit that I was surprised at the words of the princess, especially when she said that this emir said that he loved her. I was surprised because it wasn't how I imagined princesses and emirs to be when in the long winter months we would listen to the stories of the old people about kidnapped princesses and emirs wounded in the battles or because of a conspiracy. What the princess said about not wanting to be in the palace because of the pursuits of an emir who said that he loved her seemed strange to me.

"The princess could not understand how a man who loved could loan the object of his love to another.

"'This emir,' she said, 'knew what I was wearing on any given day, but when I would hide from him with all the others, he never tried to find me. When I motioned so that he would notice me, he paid no attention and would go to another. And when he saw that another hunter was coming close to me, he would whisper something into his ear and it was clear that he was showing that man where I was hiding, so that he would take me, while the emir himself took another woman. When my mother started asking me about him, I told her that I would not let anybody else get close to me, that I was sick of everything, that I could not even look at the one bearing the name of my fiancé, that I was bored with the quietness of the palace, its food, clothes, and relationships. That is why I went where a person is closer to Allah, the earth, and the people: to the country, and your house was the closest place to the palace. And if I could choose, I perhaps would say that you are the closest to my soul.'

"Having said that, she started crying so that my mother started kissing her on her head to relieve her suffering and kept telling her that the emir was a miserable coward and a villain. Then she sat down by her and asked, 'Could it be, my dear, that you are only imagining all this about this emir? What if he failed to find you by mistake and not on purpose?'

"Then my mother said, 'As your sister, I cannot understand how your fiancé, the emir, if he says that he loves you, could take part in such games? Isn't a man a fortress and a wall around a woman? But this scoundrel behaved himself in such a way that he became not a wall but the gates of hell for you.'

"When my father joined the conversation, my mother said, 'She started to hate everything in her life, to hate all the things she was given. They treated her as if she were a hen, which the old woman keeps in the hen-house in fear that a coyote or a fox might attack them. The old woman feeds the hens and gives them water and either takes the eggs or leaves them in their nests, and then they have little chicks.'

"The princess cried out in despair, 'Yes, we became like hens, but if the old woman was guarding her chicks from the fox, those who guard us are locking us up in the palace not because of the foxes and coyotes, but to isolate us from the people, so that we do not pick up their ideas and would not know about their life. They do all this to us under the excuse of maintaining the traditions of the palace, the traditions of the kings and emirs. That is why your life resonates in my soul. It seems to me that it is close to my soul. It is in my soul. Can a human being say that she lives if she does not smell the aroma of earth, the smell of a real man, as he is, if she does not make food with her own hands, does not put her own clothes on, if she does not wash her body without watchers and helpers? The life in the palace is full of fake images and flowers. The air is caught between the thick walls, and even the animals that live in the palaces are different from the wild animals, who reflect in themselves all the richness and vividness of nature.'

"Do you understand, O miserable man," said the woman to the landowner who was speaking before her, "that the new regime deserves to be a regime of the people?"

Then he answered her, "Yes, because among them there are noble people, like the princess who came to you and whom you told us all about."

The woman said, "I did not say that there are no noble people in the royal regime, but I am saying that this regime is not capable of strengthening and unifying the people, from those who live in the main royal palace to the lowliest of servants. And most of all, it does not provide for the strength and protection of the people. If there are some exceptions among the emirs and princesses, like the princess I was talking about, they are very rare. So can we establish the law and the government based upon the exceptions, or should we rely on the majority when we make decisions? Is it right to put people in a position of uncertainty when it is never known who will inherit the power of his father, even if the present king who holds the power is good? Do you, most respectable landowner, want your house to have a fence around it with a door, the key to which would be in your possession, or do you want some-

thing else? We want it so that the people would become a fence for the country and so that the key to
that fence was in trustworthy hands, the hands of
one who knows the people. We want the people to
be able to choose, through constructive meetings,
who would be good for it. That way, the government
will not be established under the influence of
money or social standing. We want it so that the
main basis for the choice is not a hereditary right,
but personal qualities, fitness of that man for the
position, and his abilities to accomplish certain responsibilities. What would you prefer, most respectable landowner, that your cow would bear
from a bull whose pedigree is well known for the
abundance of meat and milk, or would you rather
have her bear from a bull of unknown pedigree?"

The landowner asked, "What do you mean by
that?"

"If you don't know what I mean, what right
do you have to possess all the lands that you have,
where people labor as if they were slaves? Are a cow
and a bull not a part of reality in a peasant's life
like a king and a queen are the reality of the royal
regime, which you wish to flourish? We do not
know about the family of the uncles of our kings on
their mother's side, most respectable landowner,
and at this time we do not even know of the pedigree of the uncles from the father's side either, as
we do not know the family of the maid of that Jew
which was given as a present for your father."

"What difference does it make for you, a
common woman, what roots I have?" asked the
landowner.

The soldier of the resistance, whose name
was Zahra, answered him, "You are right, I am a
daughter of the common people, but I am the
daughter of a man whom everybody knows. Everybody knows his character and his roots. I am a

daughter of a man from the people and everybody knows who he is. People know the family of my father, my grandfather, my uncle, and his father and grandfathers, and so I can tell you the names of all of my grandfathers and all kinds of uncles up to the fiftieth generation. And what about you, can you tell me the names of your grandfathers and uncles, at least to the third generation?"

"Is that important for the power structure?"

"Yes, it is important, because a good tree bears good fruit and a bad tree bears bad fruit. The man who doesn't know his uncles and brothers is not bothered if others do not know their roots either. Under the cover of a blood relationship, a foreigner could infiltrate the government and reign over our people and our nation. And then his reign would be a road to shame and humiliation, not to greatness and glory, and his reign would provide no protection for the state. And another matter is whether the ruler is educated and trustworthy. Also, I wanted to ask you, is the son of somebody that had great power more courageous on the battlefield than a son of the poor?"

"What do your words mean?"

"My words mean a lot for the conclusion we have come to in our conversation."

The landowner said, "So the main thing is education and up-bringing. In how the father brings up his son."

And she added, "What's important is education and environment."

The landowner answered, "Yes, and environment."

Then she asked, "And did you raise your sons so that they became soldiers, as it is proper?"

He answered, "I brought up the peasants on my land and they constitute a much larger force than one of my sons ever would. Those peasants became very good fighters. They are protecting their land, and the army benefits from them greatly."

"You did not prepare them for the army. It is poverty that made them what they are, and also their own ideals and customs which form their souls and minds. The luxury of your home did not allow your sons to become good warriors. Luxury did not allow them to find out what life is and to taste it, and their mother did not teach them patriotism or the national ideals of *our* country and *our* people. Even worse, the nurses of your children are foreigners and their teachers are from abroad. Also, because you teach them to read and write in imitation of the kings and emirs in this kingdom and neighboring kingdoms, they cannot lead armies to fight for our honor. We do not expect courage from them since they have removed themselves from us and from our God. The princess I told you about now lives in our house where she found protection. We keep her and protect her, and she lives with us. We consider her our older sister, so that neither you nor anybody else could say that the common people are not capable of loyalty and gratitude, after you made all your money by exploiting us, the money that killed both your conscience and honor. And if you want to convince the women who took part in the resistance," she said firmly, "that we have to maintain the royal regime and leave you all of your land that you have stolen in the same way that your father stole it from our people, giving away the rich garments and jewelry of your wives to find our favor, I think that you will not be able to convince very many of us. But if you distribute what the kings and emirs have to the people, if you give away what the merchants earned dishonestly and all that you have, you will become our first candidate for leading the new government. We will surround you like walls, protecting you and supporting you. Are you ready to disappoint those who are a part of this rotten system? Are you ready for decisive actions which will allow neither compromise nor uncertainty?"

An explosion of applause followed her words, and after that, shouts could be heard, praising the people and praising the glorious heroines and heroes and praising the army. There were also curses toward cowards and traitors, those who had gained their fortunes at the expense of the people.

*** 

So they were sitting in the hall, when a man rushed in and whispered something in the ear of the chairman of the council.

The chairman of the council announced the news, "We all come from Allah and we all go back to him. Allah has settled what we could not settle and he is the best judge. The chief servant from the palace has just informed me that the king is dead! Truly, death is just. It is our responsibility to accompany the one who was the king of our country into his last journey, first of all to give him what is due; second, to follow the tradition which is pleasing to Allah. All the people must join the procession. Then, we will come back to discussing our plans and we will continue to do so with renewed energy and with a new spirit.

"May Allah be merciful to all who have died!

"Praise to the martyrs!

"Praise to Zabiba!

"Long live Zabiba!

"Long live the people!

"Long live the army!"

Printed in December 2023
by Rotomail Italia S.p.A., Vignate (MI) - Italy